Rio Renegade

*Also by Leslie Ernenwein
in Large Print:*

Bullet Breed
Gunhawk Harvest
Rampage
Trigger Justice

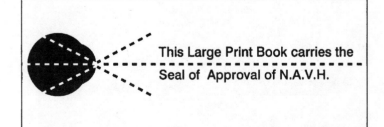

Rio Renegade

Leslie Ernenwein

WHEELER
PUBLISHING

Published in 2005 by arrangement with
Golden West Literary Agency.

Wheeler Large Print Western.

The text of this Large Print edition is unabridged.
Other aspects of the book may vary from the original edition.

Set in 16 pt. Plantin by Minnie B. Raven.

Printed in the United States on permanent paper.

Library of Congress Cataloging-in-Publication Data

Ernenwein, Leslie.
    Rio renegade / by Leslie Ernenwein.
        p. cm. — (Wheeler publishing large print westerns)
    ISBN 1-58724-903-0 (lg. print : sc : alk. paper)
    1. Mexican American Border Region — Fiction.
    2. Large type books.   I. Title.   II. Wheeler large print
    western series.
    PS3555.R58R56 2005
        813´.54—dc22   2004025725

Rio Renegade

As the Founder/CEO of NAVH, the only national health agency solely devoted to those who, although not totally blind, have an eye disease which could lead to serious visual impairment, I am pleased to recognize Thorndike Press★ as one of the leading publishers in the large print field.

Founded in 1954 in San Francisco to prepare large print textbooks for partially seeing children, NAVH became the pioneer and standard setting agency in the preparation of large type.

Today, those publishers who meet our standards carry the prestigious "Seal of Approval" indicating high quality large print. We are delighted that Thorndike Press is one of the publishers whose titles meet these standards. We are also pleased to recognize the significant contribution Thorndike Press is making in this important and growing field.

Lorraine H. Marchi, L.H.D.
Founder/CEO
NAVH

★ Thorndike Press encompasses the following imprints: Thorndike, Wheeler, Walker and Large Print Press.

Chapter 1

A plume of sun-sparkled dust rose above the barren flats just west of Reservation. It travelled out into breeze-blown streamers that drifted across Main Street and finally settled against Cemetery Hill at the north end of town. There was a pattern of premonition in the dust's journey — a kind of sign that men might read. But the three men on the Palace Hotel's second-floor gallery weren't watching the dust; they were watching the ten riders behind it.

Jim Fayette, youngest of the trio on the gallery, said: "Shad Harlequin believes in coming to town well heeled. He's got the pick of his slug slammers with him."

Fayette, ramrod of Pardee-Shannon's big Spur spread, looked as gaunt as one of Spur's slat-ribbed steers. Ten months of drought and toil and frugal living on the Border Desert range had honed him down. Those months had put a questing squint in his smoke-blue eyes and stamped haggard lines on his angular, sun-blackened face. But they hadn't shrunk his devil-be-damned grin nor changed the rash ways of his thinking.

"Harlequin always did like lots of company," Branch Shannon reflected, and glanced at Dobie Dan Pardee, who'd been his partner for twenty years. "Far back as I can remember, Shad Harlequin never rode alone."

"I can recall when he did most of his riding in the dark of the moon," old Dobie Dan declared, sitting with his saddle-warped legs astraddle of a chair. "Mark my words, Branch — we'll have to fight Shad Harlequin and his Bootjack bunch no matter which way the trial goes tomorrow. You can be damned sure of that!"

They looked a lot alike, these two old Texans who'd migrated west at the end of Lee's lost rebellion. But actually they were direct opposites in many ways, for Shannon had the conservative code of a cautious, peace-loving business man, whereas Dobie Dan belonged to the hell-for-leather breed of cowman who considered a Colt revolver the best court of appeal.

Glancing at these partners now, and comparing them with Shad Harlequin, who was leading his riders along Main Street, Jim Fayette felt a strong sense of apprehension. There'd been a time when Pardee-Shannon ruled the roost in this end of Arizona Territory. But that day was gone. Bootjack was the big outfit now, its line camps controlling a far-flung cattle kingdom that made even Spur's vast holdings a poor second. Using all the tricks of political bribery, night riding and mysterious murder, Harlequin had driven a hundred-mile wedge between Spur's Border Desert range and its headquarters here in the north — a wedge that spelled ruin — if it stuck.

"I still think we should've jumped Harlequin when he first started crowding the small outfits off the Spanish Grant," Fayette said quietly, well knowing how ticklish a subject this was with Branch Shannon. "There was just one reason Harlequin wanted that sorry strip of country — so he could close the Spanish Grant Trail and blockade Spur out of business."

Branch Shannon lit a fresh cigar and considered Fayette with an old man's tolerance. He said finally: "Just because your fast fanning of a six gun once saved Dan from being dobie-walled down in Sonora doesn't mean that every problem can be solved with slugs. This isn't Mexico, and it's no Border Desert. We've got law courts up here."

"Tin-star law and crooked courts!" Dobie Dan snorted contemptuously. "They're controlled by Shad Harlequin, so what the hell good are they, Branch? Ain't no justice in 'em at all!"

"Perhaps not," Shannon admitted patiently. "But they're a start in the right direction, Dan — in the only direction that means survival for legitimate cowmen doing an honest business. Men of Harlequin's stripe won't always be able to steal elections and put crooks no better than themselves into office. The day will come when we'll have real law in this country."

A cynical smile quirked Jim Fayette's long lips. "By that time Spur's south range will be a boneyard," he muttered. "The Rio Pago went dry two weeks ago. In another month there'll be dust in half the tanks and water holes from Apache Flats to Sonora."

Shannon frowned and asked, "Bad as that?"

"Yeah," Dan Pardee grumbled, "and it'll be worse before it's better. If we don't git rain down there *muy pronto,* we'll have to drive everything north this year. Not just beef steers, but breeder stock and calves —

the whole damn caboodle!"

Shannon, who ran Spur's headquarters ranch in the Tonto country north of Reservation, seldom saw the Border Desert range any more. But because he kept Spur's tally books, he knew within a hundred how large a trail herd such a drive would involve. "Upwards of five thousand head," he mused scowlingly.

Then he asked, "Did you find that deed to the Spanish Grant Trail, Dan?"

Pardee nodded. He patted his hip pocket and chuckled. "Shad Harlequin will be considerable surprised when I spring it in court tomorrow. Funny thing is, I'd of been satisfied with a jawbone agreement from Fonso Chavez fifteen years ago when I dickered for that right-of-way across his land. But old Fonso was tol'able proud of bein' able to write English, so he ciphered it all out in ink, purty as you please."

Jim Fayette watched the Bootjack bunch dismount at Jock Gilligan's Livery farther down the street. And because he shared Dobie Dan's dislike for law courts, he gave Harlequin's riders a calculating appraisal. There was no doubt that the hawk-faced owner of Bootjack had hired a hard-case crew. For even though Fayette recognised only three of them — Red Bastable, Harlequin's beefy, buck-toothed foreman; Kid Carmody, who'd ridden with the Wild Bunch in Texas; and the Mexican, Breed Santana — the others bore the same slug-slammer brand. They made an impressive show of strength, those ten gun-hung men; a threatening, convincing show that had political power behind it.

Fayette was thinking about that, and making a mental tally of all the other riders on Bootjack's big payroll, when the screen door opened behind him and he turned to see Sheriff Jube Frobisher in the gallery doorway.

"Howdy, men," was the greeting of the big-bellied lawman, whose spongy face had its usual whisky-flush.

Branch Shannon said civilly, "Hello, sheriff."

But Dobie Dan didn't speak. He just stared at the lawman, and so did Fayette.

"Came up to tell you men I'm making a special rule in the interests of law and order," Frobisher announced pompously. "From now until the trial is over, everybody has to check their guns. I don't want no shootin' scrapes to spoil the legal show-down between Spur and Bootjack."

"Good idea," Shannon agreed, plainly pleased.

"Spur will obey the rule one hundred per cent. You can be sure of that."

"So will everyone else," Frobisher declared, and turned back into the hotel.

The thought occurred to Jim Fayette that Frobisher stepped lightly for so big a man, making scarcely a sound as he walked along the hallway. That fact seemed to hold some remote significance, but Fayette couldn't identify it. And presently, seeing Gail Shannon come out of the Bon Ton Millinery, he forgot all about the sheriff.

She was something to see, this sorrel-haired daughter of Branch Shannon — something to stir a man's blood — especially when he hadn't seen her for almost three months. Remembering back to their first meeting, Fayette smiled reflectively. He'd been new on Spur's payroll then, and didn't know that Gail was practically engaged to young Keith Fabian, who'd inherited a bank from his father. When Gail turned down his invitation to attend a dance at Odd Fellows Hall that evening, he had hidden his disappointment by taking Doc Nelson's dusky-haired daughter to the dance. But later, when he'd finally got to waltz with Gail, something had happened to him — something that was like hunger and thirst and being drunk, all at the same

13

time. And, strangely enough, Gail had seemed to feel the same way.

Fayette grinned, remembering. He got up and said casually, "Reckon I'll take a little look around."

"Don't forget to leave your gun at the desk downstairs," Shannon reminded him. Then, catching sight of his daughter on the sidewalk, he exclaimed, "So that's it!"

Fayette grinned and went quickly inside.

Whereupon Dobie Dan said: "They'll make a fine pair, Branch. I'll be glad to see 'em git hitched, bein' as how Jim is the nearest thing to a son an old bachelor ever had."

"I suppose they'd get married whether we liked it or not," Shannon reflected. He glanced over at the Cattlemen's Bank, where Keith Fabian stood in the doorway talking to Belle Nelson. "It's hard to feel sure about a fellow you haven't known very long, Dan. I'd — well, I'd sort of hoped Gail would marry young Fabian, who she grew up with."

Then he added thoughtfully: "Jim has made Spur a good ramrod, Dan. I've got to admit that. And he's got over his habit of gambling like a professional tin-horn every time he gets to town. But I'm remember-ing that they called him 'Fanner' Fayette

14

down in Sonora before he went to work for us."

Dan Pardee grinned. "Hell, Jim was just a harum-scarum kid takin' a looksee over the hill. That was five years ago, Branch, and Jim is only twenty-four now. An orphan with no strings on him was bound to go fancy-dancin' through the hills, admirin' of his shadder until the time came to settle down. Just like a fiddle-footed colt. But Jim chucked his renegade ways the day he signed on with Spur."

"So be it," Shannon said, and taking a tally book from his pocket, scanned a complicated set of figures. "The drought has hurt us bad, Dan. Our calf crop has shrunk steadily for three years, and that's knocked our beef production down fifty per cent. On top of that, we had to buy feed to get through the winter, which practically wiped out our bank balance. If we bid in that contract to deliver beef to the railroad construction camp at Tonto Junction, I'll have to plaster a mortgage on Spur to raise the cash forfeit they'll demand."

Pardee shrugged, as he always did when money matters came up. "You do it any way that looks best to you," he suggested. "No use worryin' about it yet, nohow. We ain't corralled the contract, and I got a sneakin' hunch Harlequin won't let us underbid him. Not if he knows we're hard up for cash. He'd figger the railroad deal might put us back on our feet — which is the one thing he won't let happen if he can help it."

Then Pardee asked, "You sendin' Gail to that summer school, same as last year, Branch?"

"Yes," Shannon muttered. "It's a promise I made Mary before she died. And I've got to keep it — no matter what happens."

"You sure as hell have," Pardee agreed.

Chapter II

Down on the hotel steps, Jim Fayette watched Gail Shannon come along the sidewalk — seeing the familiar and lovely picture she made. Gail wore a perky little black hat tilted forward on her blonde hair, and a velvet dress that was the exact blue-grey color of campfire smoke on a windless morning. She stopped to chat with Effie Sprague, and during this interval, while Fayette waited, Pancho Garcia stepped up to the hotel veranda with a small silver trinket in his hand.

"Good-luck charm," the ragged little urchin said eagerly. "You buy heem, *Senor* Jeem?"

Fayette grinned, recalling the other times this same Pancho had sold him good-luck charms made from peso silver by a widowed mother and supposedly blessed by the mission *padre*.

"I lost fifty dollars playing poker right after I bought the last one," Fayette said with mock gravity.

"But weethout eet you would 'ave lose

much more *dinero*," the lad declared craftily. "Perhaps one 'undred dollars. Thees one ees — how you say? — the spashal charm. Weel breeng you *mucho fortuna!*"

Something in the boy's wistfully pleading eyes made Jim Fayette remember another boy — an orphan who'd had to shift for himself in a Texas cowtown — the kid they later called "Fanner" Fayette in Mexico. That kid had acquired his first pair of spurs by taking them from the heels of a drunken cowboy spraddled out behind a saloon; he'd spent most of his first years' wages buying bullets for the target practice that had made him an expert gunslinger at the age of sixteen.

Fayette took the charm, and was handing Pancho two silver dollars when Shad Harlequin led his Bootjack crew along the sidewalk.

"*Muchas gracias!*" Pancho exclaimed, so excited at receiving the extra dollar that he tripped as he went down the steps and would have fallen except that he bumped into Shad Harlequin.

The collision brought an angry curse from the Bootjack boss. "You stinkin' beggar brat!" Harlequin snapped, and grasping Pancho's arm, slapped the kid's face.

18

The impact of Harlequin's hand sounded loud to Jim Fayette, and the whimper that came from Pancho's lips brought flashing memories of his own hard-scrabble boyhood. Bitter, brutal memories.

He said sharply, "Take your hands off him, Harlequin!"

Astonishment bugged Harlequin's black eyes. He stared up at Fayette as if bewildered — as if unable to comprehend such words, or the reason they'd been uttered. Men didn't speak to Shad Harlequin in that tone of voice. He handed out the orders in this country. Nobody jawboned him — not if they knew who he was. And this Spur ramrod knew!

"You gone loco?" Harlequin demanded.

He was a full head shorter than Fayette, and lean as a lath. But an ingrained arrogance added inches to his stature, and the hard-case riders with him now increased his bully courage. "You must be plain loco!" he declared.

"Mebbeso," Fayette drawled, coming down the steps. "But I'm telling you to turn the kid loose and do it damn quick!"

Which was when Branch Shannon leaned over the upper railing and called urgently, "Wait a minute, Jim — take it easy!"

But Fayette wasn't waiting. In two long strides he reached Shad Harlequin, knocked the cattle king's hand loose from Pancho's sleeve and said rashly, "If you want to slap somebody around, take a try at me."

And in this same instant, as he stood with cocked fists ready to smash Harlequin's high-beaked face, Fayette heard Dobie Dan yell, "Look out for Bastable!"

Fayette turned in time to see Red Bastable swing. He tried to block the blow. But he didn't have time. Bastable's knuckles exploded against his jaw with an impact that sent him reeling off the sidewalk.

For a strangely suspended interval, Jim Fayette had no clear impression of what was happening. He was remotely aware of excited voices round about, of fists battering his face, and the smell of boot-churned dust in his nostrils. But because that first sneak blow had put a dancing haze in front of his eyes, Fayette couldn't see Bastable's swinging fists at all. He could only feel them.

Backing blindly with each successive blow, Fayette retreated down Main Street like a drunkard desperately trying to stay on his feet. Vaguely, as from a far distance, he heard a man yell, "Knock him down, Red!" and heard Bastable gloat, "Not till I've spoiled his handsome face some more."

That didn't make sense to Fayette — until he became aware of blood's warm wetness on his face and its salty taste in his mouth. Then he understood that Red Bastable was deliberately prolonging this one-sided spectacle for the amusement of his Bootjack cronies — and for his own enjoyment.

Presently some of the haze cleared from Fayette's eyes and he caught a blurred glimpse of Bastable's grinning face in front of him. He saw blood-smeared fists poised for swinging. He swivelled sideways in time to evade them, and taking advantage of this momentary respite, staggered away from Bastable, as if endeavouring to escape through the yawning doorway of Gilligan's Livery.

"He's running away!" Kid Carmody howled.

That taunting voice brought a twisted grin to Fayette's battered lips. Running, hell! All he wanted was a little time. Just time enough for his eyes to focus properly — for his shock-fogged senses to regain some semblance of normal perception. If he could circle Bastable, perhaps that would give him time enough. But even as he tried, he knew it was futile. Red Bastable was taking no chances; the Bootjack foreman was charging in for the kill!

Turning swiftly, Fayette met that charge head on, driving his left shoulder against the redhead's broad body and smashing a right to his beard-bristled chin. But there was no power in the blow. Bastable's bucktoothed grin jeered at him. And Bastable's sledging fists hammered him back. They were like clubs, those fists. They knocked his head from side to side. They put a roar in his ears that was like the thudding of a hundred hammers.

"How you like it?" Bastable taunted, shifting his attack to Fayette's midriff until Jim's guarding arms came down.

Fayette wheeled and turned and tried to target Bastable's buck-toothed face. But blood ran into his eyes, blinding him. Then he tried to go into a clinch. It was no use. Bastable's sledging fists hammered him back, again and again. Then something ex-ploded against his ear with a paralysing impact.

Whereupon Jim Fayette fell like a broken reed.

Red Bastable peered down at him. "Git up and fight!" he ordered gloatingly. Then he aimed a boot at Fayette's unmoving body.

"Shame on ye!" Jock Gilligan blurted, crouching beside Fayette in time to take the kick on his own rump. "Can't ye see the poor lad is licked?"

Bastable grinned. He wiped his bloody knuckles on his pants, and ignoring Dan Pardee, who came running from the hotel, joined his Bootjack comrades. "Guess I fixed Fayette's piano for him," he bragged.

"You sure as hell done it up fancy!" said Kid Carmody, praising him and admiring a brute strength his frail body didn't possess. "You fixed him proper!"

And Shad Harlequin said: "That was a fine sight to see, Red. It calls for a drink."

Then, as Branch Shannon and his daughter came along the sidewalk, Harlequin tipped his hat with exaggerated courtesy to Gail. She ignored his gesture, but Shannon acknowledged it by saying, "Howdy, Harlequin."

"Seems like your range foreman was a trifle on the prod," Bootjack's boss suggested.

Shannon frowned. He said: "That was a personal matter on Jim's part, Harlequin.

23

It had nothing to do with Spur. We aren't looking for trouble."

"Well, now," Harlequin exclaimed, "that's just dandy!"

He was plainly enjoying this conversation. He smacked his thin lips and said, "It would be a shame to let anything upset our case in court tomorrow, wouldn't it, Shannon?"

Gail stood a little to one side, urgently aware of Red Bastable's brazen appraisal. She tried to stare him down, but the Bootjack foreman ogled her with a probing intensity that seemed to penetrate her clothing.

"I'll have a talk with Fayette," said her father to Harlequin. "There'll be no more trouble before the trial."

Then he escorted her towards the livery, saying: "Jim deserved what he got. He had no right to pick a fight with Harlequin at a time like this."

And because Gail knew how useless words would be, she said nothing at all.

The Bootjack crowd went on to the Blue Bull Saloon. Harlequin handed his red-headed foreman a ten-dollar gold piece, saying, "Buy the boys a few drinks." Then he crossed the street to where Keith Fabian stood in the Cattlemen's Bank doorway.

Medium tall and fashionably garbed, the yellow-haired banker had the look of a peaceful, progressive young businessman. Which he was. "Looks like Fayette got a thorough whipping," he said as Harlequin joined him.

Shad Harlequin asked slyly: "That didn't hurt your feelings none, did it?"

"No," Fabian admitted. "I've never liked Fayette."

"Guess you got reasons for disliking him," Harlequin said. "If he'd took my gal away from me, I'd hate his damned guts."

Then, lowering his voice, the Bootjack boss said: "Spur is on the rocks financially, Keith. As a depositor in your bank, I'm warning you not to take any more Spur paper. The Pardee-Shannon outfit is done for in this country, unless they win the trial tomorrow. And I'm saying they won't win it!"

"What," Fabian asked, "makes you so sure?"

Harlequin chuckled. He said: "Never mind the how of it. I've got Pardee-Shannon in a tight fix they can't wriggle out of. They're licked!"

Keith Fabian watched Shannon and his daughter go into the livery stable. He said, "A banker has to remain neutral in range feuds, and I'm taking no sides. But I hate to see Branch Shannon go broke."

Then he added regretfully, "There was a time when I thought Branch was going to be my father-in-law."

"But you let Fayette beat you out of the fanciest filly in Arizona, just because you wouldn't stand up and fight for her," Harlequin declared. "Well, I'm not letting him and Dan Pardee beat me out of Bootjack — which is what they've got in mind. I've got 'em in a corner and I'm keeping 'em there. Six months from now there'll be just one big outfit in this end of Arizona — Bootjack. Don't forget that the next time Shannon wants to borrow money!"

Then Harlequin strode towards the Blue Bull, his silver-studded spurs jingling musically. He carried himself in the fashion of a man who possessed absolute confidence and power aplenty.

Watching him, Fabian said softly: "One big outfit in six months' time. I wonder if he's right."

Chapter III

When Jim Fayette opened his eyes, he was aware of the livery stable's rank odour and a curious wetness. Then he saw Jock Gilligan standing over him with a water bucket.

The little liveryman said: "Bastable niver give ye a chance. The dirty divil sneaked up on ye!"

Almost at once then Dan Pardee came rushing up with a whisky bottle in his hand. Kneeling beside Fayette, the old cowman pulled the cork and said wheezily: "Take a swig, Jimmy boy."

Fayette hunched up on an elbow and put the bottle to his blood-crusted lips.

"How d'you feel now?" Dobie Dan asked solicitously. The alcohol's hot jolt dissolved the fuzzy feeling in Fayette's head. It made everything seem abruptly clear and all right — until he stood up. Then he felt bruised and sore and a trifle dizzy. He said: "I've felt worse and lived. But I won't feel exactly right till I make Red Bastable take a swing at me while I'm looking at him."

Which was when Branch Shannon and Gail came into the stable and Gail exclaimed: "Jim! Are you all right?"

Fayette grinned sheepishly. "I'm just dandy," he declared.

Gail came quickly to him, her slim fingers exploring a gash on his cheek. "It was awful," she murmured. "I was afraid you'd be maimed for life."

Fayette felt better then. A familiar, warming glow came over him, as it always did when she was near. But it was brief, for Branch Shannon asked censuringly, "Why did you start such a rumpus over a Mexican kid, Jim?"

Disapproval was plain in Shannon's eyes. And something else. Something like disappointment. Seeing that expression, and remembering that this man had never fully approved of his courting Gail, Fayette searched for words to answer Shannon's question — for some fitting way to explain why tyranny always roused a resentment he couldn't control. He knew it was part and parcel of his boyhood, spawned by the brutal abuse he'd rebelled against as a kid. But knowing and explaining were two different things. He couldn't put it into words.

So he said, "Reckon I just felt like fighting," and saw Shannon's frown mirrored on Gail's oval face.

"This isn't the time nor the place for fighting," Shannon protested. "We've got a good chance to win our case tomorrow, which would mean forcing Bootjack to remove its fence from the Spanish Grant Trail. But street fighting isn't going to help our case. In fact, it will prejudice the judge against us."

"Hell's bells!" Dobie Dan blurted. "Jim only done what any fit man would do, Branch!"

But Shannon shook his head. "I didn't ask you and Jim to travel all the way up here from Border Desert just to stage Good Samaritan stunts on Main Street," he declared stubbornly. "This is a legal fight that won't be won with fists or with guns. Keep that in mind, Fayette — and act accordingly."

Then he said, "Come on, Gail," and taking his daughter's arm, strode from the stable.

For a time, while Jock Gilligan went about his barn chores, Fayette and Pardee sat talking in the stable tackroom. And because they were kindred souls, disliking the restraint which Branch Shannon's peace-loving ways placed upon them, they drowned their misery with frequent tiltings of the whisky bottle.

"Branch is a good galoot," Dobie Dan explained. "Hell, there ain't a better-hearted man west of the Pecos. But he don't see things like you and me see 'em, Jim. He's hell for law and order — thinks the gungrabbin' days are over and done with. But he'll learn different. Shad Harlequin won't open the Trail to us, no matter what the judge says tomorrow. We'll have to bust Bootjack's blockade with guns or give up our south range. And I ain't givin' it up long as I got strength enough to trip a trigger!"

That declaration cheered Jim Fayette immensely. It banished the bitterness that Shannon's reprimand had put in him. Here, he knew, was the man who would beat Bootjack in the final showdown — or die in the attempt. This saddle-warped oldster would brush Branch Shannon's legal arguments aside when the time came for fighting. Dobie Dan would get the job done in the only way it could be accomplished — by meeting toughness with toughness and ramming it right down Shad Harlequin's greedy throat.

Afterwards, when they'd had supper at the cafe, Dobie Dan said: "Reckon you'll be wanting to visit with Gail, so I'll mosey over to the Belladonna and see if Poker Pat McGurk has a game goin' in the back room. I beat them boys for quite a chunk last time we was in town."

Fayette grinned. "Dab it on 'em," he urged. "I'll come over at midnight and help you tote away your winnings."

Whereupon he headed for the hotel and was passing a dark alley just beyond the Blue Bull Saloon when a man stepped out of the shadows and said quietly, "Hello, Fayette."

Not recognising the voice, Fayette halted. Habitual wariness sent his hand to holster, and for an instant, realising it was empty, he felt a swift surge of apprehension. He said, "Howdy," and peered at the dusk-veiled face, trying to identify it.

"I'm Gus Odegarde," the man said, still speaking low. "I had a little outfit on the Spanish Grant. Remember?"

"Yeah," Fayette muttered, recalling that Odegarde had asked Spur for help when Bootjack started crowding him off the grass. But Spur had refused to interfere, and recently there'd been talk that Odegarde had turned to rustling.

"I ain't got much love for Spur," Odegarde said. "But I got even less for Bootjack. And there's four or five more of us feel the same way."

"So?" Fayette prompted.

Odegarde built a cigarette and lit it, his lean, lantern-jawed face showing briefly in the match flare. "Well, it's bein' told around that if Spur loses the trial tomorrow there'll be range war in these parts. And from what I hear, Spur ain't goin' to win in court."

Thinking of the right-of-way deed in Dobie Dan's pocket, Fayette said: "I think we've got a good chance to win. A real good chance."

"Shad Harlequin don't think so," Odegarde reported, nodding at the Blue Bull's lamplit doorway, "He's over there now, braggin' that the trial won't last an hour, and offerin' odds of ten to one that Bootjack wins it."

Then he added softly: "I know where you could hire some gun riders. Real handy ones."

"Such as who?" Fayette asked.

"Such as Single-O Smith, Limpy Peebles, Monk Rodenbaugh and English Joe. Also a couple more that I disremember their brands."

Those names startled Jim Fayette. They belonged to members of the old Texas

Wild Bunch — men he'd ridden with as a kid. "Are those galoots in Arizona?" he demanded.

"Yep. Holed up in the Fandango Hills right now," Odegarde said grimly. "I been trailin' with 'em. So's Charlie Moss and Tod Foyle. A man has got to eat."

Fayette could understand that. He could understand it perfectly. He also had trailed with the Texas renegades for the same reason. And he might still be riding with them if it hadn't been for Dobie Dan Pardee. He was thinking about that, and marvelling at the change five years could make in a foot-loose rannyhan, when Odegarde asked, "How about signin' us on?"

"No use talking about it now," Fayette said. "Not till after the trial."

"But you won't win it. Nobody ever beats Harlequin in court. You ought to know that."

"This time may be different," Fayette predicted, believing that no judge could ignore the legality of Dobie Dan's deed. "If you want to win yourself some easy money, take that ten-to-one Harlequin is offering."

"Not me," Odegarde scoffed. "I wouldn't bet a busted horseshoe on Spur's chances against that crooked son. He's

33

slicker'n cow slobbers."

Then he asked, "You figger Spur might hire us if there's a range fight?"

Fayette shrugged and said, "Ask me again when the time comes."

"Mebbeso it'll come sooner'n you think," Odegarde warned, and faded back into the alley.

Fayette went on to the hotel where Gail sat with her father on the veranda. She called, "Over here, Jim," and when he'd joined them on the long bench, Branch Shannon gave him a cigar.

"Gail says I sounded a trifle sharp when I talked at the stable," the old cowman said. "Well, I don't blame you for hating Harlequin. We all hate him, Jim. But we've got to be patient."

Fayette grinned, and feeling the gentle pressure of Gail's fingers on his arm, said, "Sure — I understand."

Presently Shannon went over to the Belladonna for his evening drink and Gail murmured, "It's been a long time, Jim."

Her face was scarcely more than a vague oval in the shadows here, but Fayette could see the sweet curve of her smiling lips. The feminine fragrance of her hair was like a delicate perfume when he took her in his arms.

"Too long, honey," he agreed. "Too darn long for a fact!"

He drew her close, wanting to kiss her, but she turned her head and asked, "Will you promise me something, Jim?"

"Practically anything except a million dollars," he declared.

"It's this: don't fight again while you're in Reservation, either with your fists or with a gun."

"I promise," Fayette said, and then he kissed her with the rash eagerness of a man long lonely.

They were still sitting there on the veranda bench at midnight when Branch Shannon came from the Belladonna. "Dan is a big winner," he reported, and went on upstairs.

"It's getting awfully late," Gail murmured. "Way past my bedtime."

But she made no move to leave.

She was there beside Fayette, her head on his shoulder, when Jock Gilligan rushed up the veranda steps and blurted, "Dobie Dan is dead!"

For a startled instant Jim Fayette sat speechless. Then he jumped to his feet and grabbed Gilligan's shoulders in a grip that made the little liveryman wince. "Who — who did it?" he demanded.

"Don't know," Gilligan said. "They found Dan layin' dead in Belladonna Alley with his pockets turned out and his throat cut from ear to ear!"

Fayette stood in shocked silence, vaguely aware of Gail's anguished voice saying, "I'll go get Dad!"

He glanced bleakly at the street; watching two men carry a limp form towards Rudd's Undertaking Parlour while a small group followed. The excited babble of their voices drifted back, merging with the off-key jangle of the Blue Bull piano. Gilligan hurried into the saloon and a moment later hurried out again with Sheriff Frobisher. When they passed the Palace veranda, Fayette heard the lawman say, "Must of murdered him for his money!"

Fayette tried to build a cigarette. But his rope-callused fingers fumbled the paper, spilling the tobacco. And in this dismal moment he remembered Gus Odegarde's warning: *"Mebbeso it'll come sooner'n you think."*

Chapter IV

They buried Dan Pardee at noon, while dreary clouds hovered close and a cold rain slanted across the bleak crest of Cemetery Hill. They lowered his coffin gently, and filled the grave while a preacher's solemn voice intoned the final benediction — while men blinked in frowning silence and women sobbed softly.

When it was done, when there was nothing left to do for the big-hearted old Texan who'd liked to ride fast with the wind in his face, they went back down the hill. All but Jim Fayette, who stood beside the wooden cross, and Branch Shannon, who sat in the livery rig waiting with his daughter.

"Jim, you'd better come now," Gail called finally.

But Fayette shook his head. "Don't wait for me," he muttered.

Branch Shannon got out of the rig and came over to Fayette, placing a hand on his shoulder. "I know how you feel, son. But there's nothing more we can do here. They refused to postpone the trial, which means we're due at court in half an hour."

"Court, hell!" Fayette exclaimed. "What difference will that make now, without the right-of-way deed they stole from Dan last night?"

Shannon said patiently: "There's no proof that Harlequin had anything to do with Dan's death. He didn't know there was such a deed. He couldn't possibly have framed Dan's death on that account. Dan had over three hundred dollars in poker winnings with him when he left the Belladonna. That'd be enough to tempt some roustabout into laying for him and taking everything Dan had in his pockets."

"Maybe," Fayette admitted, seeing the logic of Shannon's argument even though he couldn't quite believe it. "Anyway, I'm not leaving here just yet. I want to stay with Dan a little longer."

Shannon seldom cursed. But he did now. "Damn it to hell!" he muttered, glancing down at the fresh-filled grave. "Damn it all to hell!"

Then he went back to the rig, keeping his head turned so that Gail wouldn't see the tears in his eyes.

It was getting dark when Jim Fayette trudged down Cemetery Hill. A gusty wind, raw with spring's last coldness, swept slanting sheets of rain against him; window lamplight cast its yellow shine on pools of water in Main Street, and hock-deep mud sucked at his boot heels as he crossed Belladonna Alley.

This was suppertime, and the Belladonna bar was deserted save for Poker Pat McGurk. The craggy-faced saloonman took one look at Fayette and reached for his private bottle of bourbon. He poured two drinks, propped his big belly on the bar's bevelled edge and said sadly: " 'Tis a dark and dismal day, me lad. A dark and dismal day."

Fayette nodded, rain water dripping from his soggy hatbrim. He asked, "Who d'you reckon did it, Pat?"

McGurk shrugged his round shoulders. He toyed with his down-swirling moustache and said: "Wish I could give ye so much as a hint. In fact I'd like to lay me hands on the misbegotten son meself. They was three or four saddle bums in here last night, awatchin' of the poker game. But Frobisher says he can't find no clues that'd make him suspect them galoots — nor nobody else. What in hell could ye expect from an addle-brained badgetoter who patronises the Blue Bull in preference to a respectable establishment like mine?"

Then, as Fayette picked up his whisky glass, the saloonman raised his also and offered a toast: "To Dan Pardee, God rest his soul. To the finest friend ye could find east or west of the Pecos!"

"To Dobie Dan," Fayette acknowledged, and taking the drink at a gulp, shivered spasmodically.

McGurk filled the glasses again. He contemplated Fayette's frowning, bleak-eyed face for a long moment and said, "Ye thought a lot of him, didn't ye, lad?"

Fayette nodded. He wiped his wet hands on the inside of his riding jacket and gave his attention to shaping up a cigarette.

For a time they stood in reflective silence, having no easy way of expressing how they felt about Dan Pardee. Then McGurk said: "Bootjack won the trial, hands down. Judge claimed they was no real evidence to show Spur had any legal title to a trail across the Spanish Grant. That sort of gimmicks yer Border Desert ranch all to hell, don't it, Jim?"

"Mebbe not," Fayette muttered. "Mebbe there's another way to break Bootjack's blockade — the way Dobie Dan would've done it."

"Not with Branch Shannon in charge of

Spur," McGurk said sagely. "Branch wouldn't fight if Harlequin spit smack-dab in his eye."

Fayette walked to the batwings. Just before he went through them, he said, "If you see Gus Odegarde, tell him I'm in room number five at the Palace."

Then he tromped up Belladonna Alley to the corner and stood for a moment contemplating Main Street's dismal, deserted appearance. Yesterday there'd been dust on this street. There'd been sunshine and warmth and cheerfulness. Now there was just mud, and rain, and a cold wind blowing.

Remembering the good-luck charm he'd bought from Pancho Garcia, Fayette dug the trinket from his pants pocket and said cynically, "Good luck, hell!"

He had raised his hand to throw it into the street when something stopped him. Not superstition exactly, but a sense of loyalty to Pancho — and to the memory of a lonely kid in Texas. Later Jim Fayette would remember this moment and marvel at it. Now he merely dropped the silver trinket into a pocket of his riding jacket and forgot it.

Presently, as he started crossing towards the Palace, a group of riders came galloping along Main Street from Gilligan's Livery. It was impossible to identify their faces in this rain-slashed gloom, but he guessed who they were even before he heard Shad Harlequin's drunken laughter. The Bootjack bunch were heading for home, full of satisfaction and Blue Bull whisky. They passed so close that their broncs splashed Fayette with muddy water and he heard Breed Santana yell drunkenly: *"Vaminos, amigos!"*

The Mexican's voice reminded Fayette that there was a knife scar on Santana's face. It wasn't much of a clue; yet someone had cut Dobie Dan's throat, and Breed was the type of renegade that might use a knife. The thought came to Fayette that it would be a first-class clue if Shad Harlequin had known about the deed in Dan's pocket. But the Bootjack boss hadn't known it existed. Or had he?

Fayette was thinking about that as he walked to the hotel, endeavouring to fashion a flimsy link with some remote impression he'd had yesterday; something that seemed vaguely significant. But it was still evading him when he went upstairs to the room he and Dan Pardee had shared — and found Branch Shannon awaiting him.

"Suppose you've heard the news," Shannon said wearily.

"Yeah," Fayette muttered, shedding his wet jacket. "What do you plan to do now?"

Shannon made a futile, open-palmed gesture with his hands. "Only one thing left to do — appeal to a higher court."

"And what happens to your Border Desert ranch in the meantime?" Fayette demanded.

"May have to abandon it," Shannon said.

"Dobie Dan didn't intend to abandon it," Fayette declared, close to anger. "He told me he'd fight for it long as he could trip a trigger."

Shannon nodded. He knocked the ashes from his cigar and smoked in silence for a moment. Then he said quietly: "Dan would've done just that, but he wouldn't have won. Shad Harlequin is too big to be licked by range war, Jim. He would bankrupt us in a month's time."

"Us?"

"Yes. We're partners now, you and I," Shannon announced. "Dan didn't leave a will, but he told me a year ago that you'd inherit his half of Spur when he passed on."

That news astonished Jim Fayette. Even

though there'd been a close bond between them, he'd never thought of being Dan's heir. In fact he'd never thought about Dan dying. Not Dan Pardee, whose brag it was that he'd been born during a Comanche raid — that his mother had killed two Indians with a broom handle the same afternoon and weaned him on corn likker three days later. "Done cut my teeth on the barrel of my pappy's peacemaker," Dobie Dan used to say, "and never been sick a day in my life."

Even now, with the stark picture of Dan's coffin etched vividly in his mind, it didn't seem possible that the tough old Texan was dead — the man who'd always laughed at death and had scoffed at an Apache's poor aim while he pulled an arrow all the way through his own thigh.

Suddenly it occurred to Fayette that Dan's share of Spur wasn't the only thing he had inherited today. The old hell-for-leather cowman had left him another legacy: a heritage of hate against a range hog's blockade!

Fayette stepped over to the bureau, picked up his gun-gear and strapped it on. "Here," he said, patting the Walker model Colt, "is the court Dan would've appealed to. I feel the same way."

"What do you mean?" Shannon demanded.

"I mean to fight Bootjack for as long as I can trip a trigger," Fayette said rashly.

And when Branch Shannon tried to explain how hopeless such a war would be against Harlequin's gunslick crew, Fayette told him about Gus Odegarde's offer — about Single-O Smith, Limpy Peebles, Monk Rodenbaugh and English Joe. "Those boys are a match for Bootjack's slug-slammers," he announced.

"But they're outlaws!" Shannon objected. "Scum of the Border!"

Fayette nodded. "The kind of scum we need to beat Bootjack. You can't fight a range war with Gentle Annies. You've got to use men who know the tricks of the trade."

"Not while I own half of Spur," Shannon declared stubbornly. "I'd rather lose every cow on our south range than turn Spur into a renegades' roost for Texas outlaws!"

For a lingering moment Fayette eyed Shannon thoughtfully, knowing the old cowman wouldn't budge; that he'd stick to the law court method of fighting Harlequin no matter how long it took. Or what it cost. And he knew Shannon wouldn't win; not with the crooked courts and political grafters Bootjack controlled.

Finally Fayette said: "I'll make you a proposition, Branch. You keep your half of Spur — the big half that you won't have to fight for, right now at least. I'll take Border Desert Ranch to do with as I please."

The impact of that scoffing declaration showed plainly in Shannon's outraged voice when he demanded: "And what will you use for money? Do you realise that we've practically no cash in the bank — that the only way we'll get any is to outbid Harlequin for that railroad beef contract? You know that Andy Kane and the BD crew haven't had a payday in two months. What are you going to pay them with if we split Spur?"

"I'll bring a beef herd through Harlequin's blockade," Fayette said. "Part of it will be lost on the way, but I'll sell what's left to buy bullets and pay fighting wages to my men. And I'll battle Bootjack from hell to breakfast and back again. I'll give Harlequin the same treatment he handed the Spanish Grant squatters. I'll raid his linecamps and burn his hay and stampede his stock in the dark of the moon."

For the second time this day Branch Shannon cursed. Then he slammed his cigar into a cuspidor and exclaimed,

"You're talking like a damned Rio renegade!"

"Yeah — and that's how I'm going to
fight Harlequin," Fayette muttered deci-
sively. "Like a Rio renegade!"

He hadn't heard Gail enter the room —
didn't know she was standing there behind
him until she cried, "No, Jim — no!"

Fayette turned, and seeing the expression in her startled eyes, felt black apprehension sweep through him. Until this
moment it hadn't occurred to him that he
might lose Gail; that being loyal to Dobie
Dan would cost him so high a forfeit.

"It's something I've got to do," he said,
and wanting her to understand why he
couldn't dodge this debt to a dead man,
tried to find suitable words of explanation.
"Dobie Dan wanted to stop Shad Harlequin's range-grabbing scheme two years
ago, when Bootjack started pushing the
little outfits off the Grant. But your father
talked Dan out of it. Now Harlequin is
trying to block us off the Border Desert,
and if he gets away with that, he'll start
crowding Spur here in the north. Dobie
Dan knew that, and he intended to fight.
He left me his share of Spur — and his
share of the fighting."

"But Dan wouldn't have hired notorious

outlaws," Gail objected.

Branch Shannon said, "Perhaps he would've, Gail," and shifted his glance deliberately to Fayette. "Dan hired a Texas renegade five years ago."

"Dad! That's not fair!" Gail exclaimed.

Then she came close to Fayette and said softly, pleadingly: "Don't throw away the things we talked about last night, Jim. All the plans we've made for the future. I know how much you thought of Dobie Dan, and how awful you feel about his death. But no amount of fighting will bring him back. It'll just mean more killing, more heartbreak and loss."

As always, the sense of her nearness was like a compelling magnet to Jim Fayette. She was the shape and substance of his campfire dreams — the image of all he desired. And she was the forfeit his heritage of hate would cost him. He knew that now.

"Dad's way will take longer," Gail said, "but it's the right way, Jim. The safe and legal way."

Lamplight brought out the gold flecks in her brown eyes; it put a sheen on her sorrel hair and gave her face a glowing loveliness. "Stay with Dad," she urged.

"And if I don't?"

That question seemed to startle her. It

turned her lips entirely grave, and she said: "If you don't, you'll be throwing away everything we planned, Jim. Everything."

For a hushed moment, indecision gripped Jim Fayette. He knew she meant it; knew that there could be no compromise between them. For Gail was Branch Shannon's daughter in more ways than one. She had her father's unbending pride and his stern code of honour. And she had the same deep-rooted sense of loyalty to Branch Shannon that he had to Dobie Dan; an even deeper, more natural bond, bred of close kinship and family tradition. In a showdown she would stick with her father, despite the intimate things they'd said and done last night. And this was a showdown.

Fayette heard someone walking along the hall, and wondered idly who it was. Then he said, "I'm going to do it Dan's way, Gail — regardless."

And at this very moment Gus Odegarde eased through the doorway. "Poker Pat says you wanted to see me," the lanky rider drawled.

Fayette nodded, and Odegarde asked eagerly, "Is Spur goin' to fight Bootjack now?"

"No!" Branch Shannon shouted. "Beginning right now, Fayette has no connection with Spur. I'm going to advertise that fact in the Tombstone *Epitaph* so there'll be no doubt in anyone's mind about it!"

"But I own the Border Desert spread," Fayette declared. "That outfit is going to fight. I'm offering gun wages, payable when we bring a beef herd through Bootjack's blockade. Do you suppose the Fandango Hills bunch would be interested in riding for me, Gus?"

"Hell, yes!" Odegarde exclaimed, plainly pleased. "When do we start?"

A rash, devil-be-damned grin quirked Fayette's lips. "Right now," he said, and picking up his hat and riding jacket, accompanied Odegarde out of the room without a backward glance.

Belle Nelson was sitting at the far end of the hotel lobby with Banker Keith Fabian when Fayette and Odegarde came downstairs. She eyed Fayette's frowning face as he went out at the front door, and said wonderingly, "Jim looks like he's in a fighting mood."

The blond banker shrugged. "Fayette is always ready for a fight or a frolic," he declared. "I've got an idea he won't stay with Spur very long, now that Dan Pardee is dead."

Then Doc Nelson came in carrying his medical kit in one hand and a paper-wrapped bottle in the other. "Swede Olsen's wife just had twin boys," he announced, and shook the bottle happily. "Swede's so proud he gave me this."

Belle watched her father plod up the stairs. "He'll drink it all tonight unless I watch him," she said regretfully. "Why do the darn fools hand him booze — and then complain about him being drunk!"

Whereupon she said good night to Fabian and hurried upstairs.

Chapter V

Two hours after Fayette and Odegarde left Reservation, they halted at a fork in the trail. The rain had ceased now, and a three-quarter moon shone intermittently through dispersing clouds.

Fayette scanned the muddy main trail which led due west to Harlequin's headquarters ranch, then gave his attention to the south fork. Both trails were hoof-pocked by recent travel, and he said, "Two men left the bunch here."

"They'd be headin' for Harlequin's Calico Creek linecamp," Odegarde muttered. "That used to be my place — before Bootjack pushed me off it."

"Let's have a looksee," Fayette suggested. "It's right on our way."

Later they halted again, on a wooded ridge above Calico Creek, and gave the camp a close inspection. There was no light in the small cabin, nor any sign of life except for seven horses standing in the pole corral.

"Easy place to raid," Fayette reflected.

"Yeah," Odegarde agreed. "I found that out two years ago."

A slow grin slanted across Fayette's face. He nodded at the corral and drawled: "Seems sort of cruel to keep broncs penned up that way. Let's turn the poor critters loose, Gus, so's they can hunt some grass."

"Damn good idee!" Odegarde exclaimed eagerly.

He took his gun from its holster as they rode down the ridge, and presently he kept a close watch on the cabin doorway while Jim Fayette walked his horse up to the corral gate and opened it. Then Fayette joined Odegarde behind the corral, waved his hat at the broncs and loosed a high rebel yell.

The spooked animals surged from the enclosure in a mud-splashing stampede. Whereupon Fayette and Odegarde galloped back up the ridge and when guns began blasting behind them, fired a few random shots at the cabin.

"A taste of their own medicine!" Odegarde said joyously, and wanted to increase the dosage.

But Fayette rode across the ridge, saying, "No time for it now."

Afterwards, when they'd cut the Spanish

Grant Trail, Fayette pulled up and said: "Here's where we part company, Gus. You go tell Single-O Smith and the others what's in the wind. Tell 'em my fight against Bootjack will make the barbwire war in Texas look like a Sunday school barbecue."

Odegarde grinned. "You figger mebbe there'll be a chance to bust Bootjack complete — so's me and Charlie and Tod Foyle can come back to our old spreads?"

"Sure," Fayette said confidently. "With Andy Kane and his crew at BD sticking by me, we'll have a good chance."

"You reckon they'll all stick, now that BD ain't part of Spur no more?"

Fayette nodded. "They thought a tol'able lot of old Dobie Dan. Even if it can't be proved that Harlequin framed his killing, those BD boys will figger it was a Bootjack knife that did it, same as I do. They'll stick, sure enough."

Odegarde turned his horse east, towards the Fandango Hills. "I'll talk it up big to Single-O and the others," he promised. "We should have the chore well started by the time you join us, Jim."

"*Bueno*," Fayette said, and giving the lanky rider a farewell salute, sent his bronc southward on the wide trail he'd ridden so often with Dobie Dan Pardee, towards the fence they'd cut on their way north.

That fence, Fayette guessed, had probably been repaired. But it would be cut again, many times. Only now old Dan wouldn't be here to help do it.

For a time then, as he rode through the moonlit roughs with the aroma of wet pine drifting down from the timbered ridges, Fayette thought about Dan's death, trying to get it straight in his mind. Sheriff Frobisher was telling folks in Reservation that Dan had been murdered for the money he'd won at the Belladonna; but the old cowman had made bigger wins before without being held up.

Recalling the preacher's benediction, Fayette wondered about the hereafter, and how the Big Boss would go about grading a man like Dan. The gospel-slinger had talked a lot about heaven, but Jim couldn't picture Dobie Dan in the company of angels. He could see Dan sitting high and handsome on his big steel-dust stallion, swinging a ketch-rope and cussing the cattle, or taking his ease on the front gallery at BD of an evening with his after-supper cigar. But they didn't have steel-dust studs in heaven, nor ornery cattle to cuss. Maybe they didn't even have cigars.

Perhaps, he reflected, there might be a special place where tough old Texans went when they died — some sort of Valhalla where grama grass grew stirrup-high all year round and a man could keep his arm limbered up tossing a loop at snorty steers. Maybe there was a hallway corral between heaven and hell for men like Dobie Dan — men who wouldn't fit with the culls or tally up to the fancy short-horn stuff the angels choused around.

Then Fayette got to thinking about Gail, and knew he couldn't contrive any halfway measure with her. She'd given him his choice and had come as close to outright pleading as she would ever come. Knowing that he had lost her, he knew also that Keith Fabian would renew his courtship without delay and that Branch Shannon would welcome the banker for a son-in-law.

Whereupon Jim Fayette cursed softly and hustled his horse southward.

Chapter VI

The BD headquarters was a typical desert spread. A long main building, built of dobie bricks, formed one side of a quadrangle whose other sides were made up of a bunkhouse, a blacksmith shop and a wagon shed. Beyond were the juniper post corrals, and above all this a towering windmill clanked monotonously in the evening breeze. A weather-beaten place, this Border Desert Ranch, bearing the hardscrabble look of all bachelor outfits; yet it was the nearest thing to home Jim Fayette had ever known.

Here, on the evening of the third day after leaving Reservation, Fayette talked to Andy Kane, who'd been BD's wagon boss for ten years. They sat at Dan Pardee's spur-scarred desk in a room cluttered with the old guns and broken bridles and worn-out saddle gear that Dobie Dan had never got around to discarding. Briefly — almost gruffly — Fayette told what had happened in Reservation, and what he proposed to do about it.

"You tell the boys at the bunkhouse that

57

there won't be another payday until I sell some steers," he said finally. "Don't expect I'll make much profit on this drive, but it should bring enough to pay fighting wages and buy some ammunition."

Kane's knobby face bore a well-scrubbed brightness in the lamplight, and his sparse grey hair made a silver fringe around the bald dome of his head. He didn't speak for a long moment; then he drawled: "We should of put the boots to Shad Harlequin a long time ago, Jim. Doin' it now won't bring Dan back, but mebbeso it'll make him rest a mite easier in his grave."

"Yeah," Fayette said grimly. "That's the way I figger it."

And half an hour later, when he went over to the bunkhouse, the crew voiced the same opinion to a man.

"When do we start?" Tex Trebo demanded eagerly.

"Sunup tomorrow," Fayette said, a tough grin creasing his haggard face.

He told them then that Gus Odegarde had promised the help of his outlaw friends. But he didn't explain the details of that help. It would be better, he decided, to wait and see how well the Fandango Hills deal turned out before building up what might be a false hope of success.

"Our job now is to gather a trail herd and do it fast," he said, handing Kane the list of riders he had prepared. "This is how I want the work done."

The old wagon boss dug a pair of glasses from his shirt pocket and read off the names. "Shorty Smith go to Camp Number One and help Jake Foster and Bill Edwards work their steers to Soto Sink. Tex Trebo do the same thing at Camp Number Two with Bronson and Lane. Slim Goff, Jack Hyatt and Lee Terwilliger make the gather at Galleta Breaks."

There were more names on the list — fifteen in all — the names of men who'd ridden the Border Desert with Dobie Dan for a longer time than Jim Fayette had known him; men who'd been proud to work for Spur. They wouldn't be working for Spur now, but they'd still be riding for Dan Pardee.

Fayette was thinking about that the next morning when he gave Andy Kane his final instructions and then rode northeast towards the Fandango Hills country. Bootjack would have him outnumbered by almost two to one, but Harlequin's gun-hawks wouldn't be fighting with a heritage of hate in their hearts.

During the next ten days, great plumes

of dust spiralled all across the Border Desert where riders on sweat-lathered broncs hazed beef steers out of brush-tangled canyons, off wide mesas and down rocky ridges. There'd been no rain here for months, and so the powdery dust made sun-sparkled banners against the cloudless sky — banners that could be seen and understood by distant watchers.

Far to the north and east, where the timbered hills marked the boundary of the Bootjack range, another group of hard-riding men also gathered steers. But there had been rain aplenty here, and so no revealing dust rose above the treetops. On the night of the tenth day, at a hide-out camp deep in the Fandango Hills, Jim Fayette held a council of war with the men who'd hazed upwards of two hundred Bootjack steers into a box canyon.

"Andy Kane should've started north a couple of days ago with his trail herd," Fayette announced, warming his hands at the campfire. "That means we've got to make our move right soon."

Single-O Smith said moodily, "I still don't think you'll get away with it, Jim."

He was a monstrous man, this Smith. Bristly grey whiskers shagged his jaws, and a black leather patch, with straps slanting from below one ear and across his broad forehead, covered his blind left eye.

"Why not?" Fayette asked.

"Well, in order to throw this stolen stuff in with your beef herd comin' up from Border Desert, we'll have to cross Apache Flats, and that can't be done in the dark of one night. If a single Bootjack rider sees that move, they'll guess what you're up to, and your slaughter scheme will be busted wide open."

"It was a damn fool scheme to start with," Monk Rodenbaugh complained, a scowl rutting his ape featured face. "How in hell d'you expect to run Bootjack's blockade when they can see you comin' for two days before you get there?"

"That," Fayette explained, "is part of the plan. They'll be laying for us in Spanish Canyon, which is the way Spur always went. They'll be expecting us to try it at night — and they won't be able to read brands before they start shooting. Also they won't know that only two hundred head are coming through the canyon while the BD herd goes through the fence five miles east."

For a time then, while they absorbed this explanation, the men squatting around the campfire were silent. English Joe, who'd ridden up and down both sides of the Border with a Mira music box strapped to his saddle, set the little instrument to playing *La Paloma*. The soft, melancholy music reminded Fayette of the last time he'd heard Gail Shannon play the piano. Almost a year ago, it was, and about this same time of day — while the Chinese cook at Spur washed supper dishes and Branch Shannon sat smoking with Dobie Dan on the front veranda. There'd been no real threat of impending range war then; no talk of trials, or Texas renegades. Gail had played *La Paloma* that night; she'd played *Black-eyed Susie* and *Sweet Alice Ben Bolt*, and afterwards there'd been a smile on her ripe red lips when he kissed her.

Sitting here now, with these noose-dodging renegades about him, Fayette could scarcely convince himself that all this change had taken place in a few short months. That evening at Spur seemed like a long, long time ago — too long to remember.

"Jim's scheme sounds all right to me," Gus Odegarde said presently. "I don't see nothin' wrong with it."

Charlie Moss and Tod Foyle sat by themselves over to one side. They'd been law-abiding homesteaders until six months ago, and the rustler role was plainly distasteful to them.

Now Moss asked, "Like Single-O pointed out, how we goin' to git this stolen stuff into the BD trail herd without bein' seen?"

"Yeah," Monk Rodenbaugh demanded. "How d'you figger to do that?"

Doubt had been strong in these men for days. Even though they'd agreed to steal the steers needed for Jim's blockade-running plan, they'd doubted the chances of its success. And they still did. Even Gus Odegarde wasn't too confident; but because the desire for vengeance was hot in him, Gus was eager to try anything that might hold a chance to reclaim his homestead.

There were times, like now, when Fayette had his doubts also; when the black boots of fatigue and lack of sleep tromped a bitter sense of futility into him. He'd been asaddle almost continuously for the past ten days and nights, and the strain of it was like a weighty burden on his shoulders. It was at moments like this that he remembered the shocked expression in Gail's eyes when she'd said: *You'll be throwing away everything we planned, Jim. Everything!*

He built a cigarette and lit it with a burning twig from the fire's embers. "There's a way to keep Bootjack from watching Apache Flats," he announced finally. "And it'll only take three men to do it."

"How?" Monk Rodenbaugh demanded. "How the hell could you do that with three men — or thirty?"

Whereupon Fayette revealed the part of his plan which would ignite the fuse of open range war — would start the guns blasting all across the hills.

"Harlequin will have a bunch of riders at his Calico Creek linecamp and another bunch at Chavez Corral. They'll be waiting for us to show at Spanish Canyon, planning to jump us from both sides. But they won't expect a raid at Calico Creek tomorrow morning — a three-man raid that'll keep them so busy they won't be watching the Flats."

"A case of the squeaky wheel getting the grease — in reverse," English Joe suggested.

And Single-O said: "It might work at that, Jim. It just might."

But Monk Rodenbaugh wasn't satisfied. "It still sounds loco to me," he complained. "If you're so sure you know where them Bootjack riders will be camped, why not wipe 'em out with a sneak raid and be done with it?"

"Man's inhumanity to man," English Joe said censuringly, and dodged the burning mesquite branch that Rodenbaugh threw at him.

Gus Odegarde asked, "Am I going on the three-man raid, Jim?"

Fayette smiled at the eagerness in his voice. "Yeah," he said, "and I've got a hunch you'll enjoy it."

Chapter VII

It was nearly daylight when Fayette, Odegarde and Smith halted their horses on the wooded ridge above Calico Creek. Night's dampness made a misty haze that half hid the cabin, and beyond it, where the rain-swollen creek overflowed its banks, a solid shroud of fog lay close to the ground.

Fayette peered at the yard, seeing a chuck wagon near the cabin and the dim shapes of occupied bedrolls on the ground. "Just like I figgered," he said. "Harlequin is all set to cover Spanish Canyon from both sides. There'll be another bunch camped at the old Chavez Corral west of the Grant Trail."

"Twelve bedrolls down there," Single-O Smith said. "Mebbe four or five more men bunked in the cabin."

Gus Odegarde, clumsily shaping a cigarette with cold-numbed fingers, said impatiently: "Let's start the music, Jim. It'll be full daylight in another ten minutes."

Even as Odegarde spoke, a man crawled from beneath the chuck wagon and began building a fire.

"We spread out a little, and shoot wide to wake 'em up," Fayette announced. "I don't want anybody hit down there before they've had a chance to defend themselves."

"Bootjack wasn't that particular when they drove me out," Odegarde objected, pulling his Spencer carbine from its scabbard. "We could kill some of them sons before they get shot of their blankets."

"No!" Fayette snapped. "By grab, you'll do it my way, Gus, or you won't do it at all!"

Single-O Smith chuckled in his beard. "Fanner always was hell for fighting fair," he drawled reflectively, "even in the old days, when they called him a killer. He don't talk like English Joe, but he's got the same fancy idees in his noggin."

"Fightin' fair won't git us nothin' when we're up against Shad Harlequin's gunslick bunch," Odegarde complained. "Them galoots deserve guttin' with a dull knife, Jim — every one of 'em!"

"Mebbeso," Fayette admitted. "But we're not shooting them while they're asleep, regardless."

They started spreading out then, Odegarde still grumbling and Smith wearing an amused grin. "Don't waste too much ammunition," Fayette warned. "We've got to keep that bunch busy all day."

Presently, when the horses had been tied well back in the timber, Fayette crouched behind a windfall at the rim of the ridge. This, he reflected, would give his plan a good chance for success. Keeping Bootjack occupied here today would allow Monk Rodenbaugh and his crew ample time to start the stolen steers across Apache Flats without being seen, and they should throw in with Kane's northbound herd before sunup tomorrow. After that, Bootjack could look and be damned.

Fayette watched a man carry a bucket of water from the creek. He was tentatively centering the bucket in the sights of his Winchester when Single-O Smith's rifle exploded farther along the ridge and water spouted from a hole in the bucket. Fayette grinned. Single-O had always been proud of his marksmanship. He had a right to be.

The cook dropped the bucket and raced towards the cabin with his shirttail whipping out behind him and his excited yell making remote echoes in the momentary hush that followed. Then, as both Odegarde and Smith began slamming slugs into the chuck wagon, wild confusion reigned briefly in the yard. Men scrambled frantically from bedrolls and rushed for cover, some barging into the cabin, others ducking behind it. Two riders, caught near the corral fence, hastily constructed a barricade of saddles from the kak pole.

Yet, despite the unexpectedness of this attack, Bootjack's gunhawks were forted up and firing three minutes after Smith's first bullet had ventilated the water bucket. That, Fayette reflected grimly, was as fast as a troop of well-trained cavalry could have done it; and it showed how swiftly Harlequin's slugslammers could go into action.

For a time then, the continuous explosion of those massed guns rolled up the ridge like heavy thunder, and searching slugs ripped the damp earth all along the rim. It was full daylight now, fog fading from the creek, and the first flush of sunrise tinting the eastern sky. Fayette glanced over at Gus Odegarde, who was hunkered on his heels behind a huge boulder. The lanky rider was hastily shoving fresh shells into the carbine's loading gate; when he started firing again, there was a savage, exultant expression on his long-jawed face.

Remembering that this had once been Odegarde's homestead, Fayette understood why Gus had wanted to shoot sleeping men and why he was enjoying himself so immensely now. Those Bootjack riders down there were the same as Apaches to Gus; they'd invaded his property and driven him off it by the same nefarious tricks the Indians used.

There was a momentary lull in the firing, and in this brief interval Fayette picked up a remote suggestion of hoofbeats. The sound came from his left, where the ridge swung eastward in a wide arc north of the creek. For a moment, as Fayette scanned the timbered crest, he wondered what a rider would be doing out so early in the morning. Then, suddenly, he guessed the answer: that man had been standing guard and had failed to detect their approach until the firing started. Now, cut off from camp, he was heading west — to get reinforcements from Chavez Corral!

The certainty of that sent Fayette backing away from the rim. If the Bootjack rider wasn't stopped, there'd be hell to pay here. Three men couldn't hold this ridge against attack from both sides; with Harlequin's gunhawks coming at them from all angles, the fight would not last an hour. And it must last until dark — or the plan would be a complete failure.

Single-O Smith also heard the hoof-pound, for he called, "Someone ridin' yonderly, Jim."

Fayette ran back to his bronc and leaped into the saddle. "You two keep the camp entertained while I corral that loose rider," he ordered.

Then he listened for a moment, calculating the rider's exact location. There was, he estimated, a quarter of a mile between them. The Bootjack man was a trifle east — which meant there'd be a good chance to intercept him.

Whereupon Fayette went down the west slope at a run. He crossed a three-mile clearing, rode into the timber beyond it and, pulling up, kept a close watch on the open space north of him. The guns were going again over at the creek, their distance-muffled reports sounding like the rumble of far-off thunder. But it was quiet here — so quiet that the panting of his bronc and the slight jingle of a curb chain sounded loud. Moisture dripped from pine branches that made a solid shield against morning's faint sunlight, and the damp air here retained night's coldness.

Waiting out a long five minutes without detecting either sight or sound of an oncoming horse, Fayette cursed. Perhaps he'd misjudged the angle of the Bootjack rider's travel, or else the man had changed course. Yet this was the logical route to Chavez Corral.

The vital need to locate that rider and stop him at all costs prodded Fayette on relentlessly. If, by dint of fast riding, the Bootjack gunhawk had succeeded in crossing the meadow ahead of him, there was no time to lose. Each moment he waited here would widen the breach between them; unless he found the tracks within a matter of minutes, there'd be no chance of catching up.

Impatience pulled hard at Fayette's fatigue-frayed nerves. But because he had a gambler's habit of relying on his judgment, he waited another long moment — and was rewarded by seeing the Bootjack rider start across the clearing directly towards him!

A rash grin loosened Fayette's lips. He slid his Winchester into his saddle scabbard and, drawing his six gun, checked its loads. That bronc was coming fast, being spurred unmercifully by a rider bent low in the saddle.

When the rider was less than a hundred yards away, Fayette recognised the pock-marked face and slight form of Kid Carmody. And a few moments later, as the Kid came close, Fayette called sharply, "Reach, Kid — reach high!"

Carmody yanked his horse back so hard that the animal slid on its haunches with its front feet off the ground. And in this fleeting moment, while the bronc's rearing body formed a broad shield, Kid Carmody's gun exploded.

That bullet smashed into Fayette's right thigh with an impact that knocked him sideways in the saddle. It made his first shot miss by a wide margin, and when Carmody's second slug creased the rump of Fayette's horse, the animal went into a tantrum of bucking.

The bronc's frenzied gyrations spoiled Fayette's aim as he tried to target Carmody, but its pitching also saved Fayette from slugs the Bootjack rider kept slamming at him. One of those bullets ripped bark from a tree so close to Fayette's face that slivers slashed his cheek; another cut a red rut across his horse's neck, taking a hank of hair with it.

Fayette gritted his teeth against the pain that stabbed his right leg with each jolting jump. Narrowly avoiding collision with trees, crashing through brush and windfalls, he fought the spooked bronc into submission. And then, scanning the timber, he loosed a croaking curse. Kid Carmody was nowhere in sight. The Bootjack gunhawk was gone — *vamoosed!*

It didn't occur to Jim Fayette that he'd missed death by a feather-fine margin, nor that the bloody wound in his leg needed attention. All he thought about now was that he'd had Kid Carmody within easy shooting distance and had failed to stop him; that he'd bungled the one chore that might mean salvation for a blockaded beef herd.

Cursing himself for a fair-fighting fool who'd given the Kid a chance to surrender instead of blasting him down from ambush, Fayette searched for Carmody's tracks and soon found them. His sweat-lathered bronc, winded by its long and violent pitching, was in no condition for fast riding. Carmody, Fayette guessed, had a reasonably fresh horse under him and at least a mile head start. There wasn't a chance of overtaking him. Not a Chinaman's chance!

Yet, even then, with splinters of pain spiraling up from his wound and a slogging sickness clutching at his stomach, Fayette didn't quit. There might be a bare possibility of keeping the Kid within rifle range — of getting a distance shot at him in the next clearing.

With that frugal hope shaping a frail barrier against the dismal sense of futility in him, Fayette followed the fresh tracks westward, mile after mile. Doggedly, desperately — as he'd done so many times riding with the Wild Bunch in Texas — he kept his tired bronc at a run, slowing only often enough to conserve the ebbing reservoir of its endurance. And because Fayette's leg was now sheathed by a wooden numbness, he no longer felt the sharp splinters of pain — only a throbbing ache — and the warm wetness of blood that kept running down into his boot.

Crossing a dry wash between two wooded hills, Fayette scanned the tracks here. They had been made so recently that small particles of dust still sparkled in the sunlit air. And then he saw something else — something that brought a swift surge of savage satisfaction. There was a brownish smear on the sand — the tell-tale stain of blood!

Instantly he realized that one of his shots had tallied. One of those hurried, half-aimed slugs had hit Carmody — or his horse. There were more stains on the rocks beyond the wash, and the sight of them roused a higher and higher eagerness in Jim Fayette. Maybe there was still a chance to keep Kid Carmody from delivering his message to the Bootjack bunch at Chavez Corral. A good chance.

Rushing his bronc up through the pines, Fayette scanned the timber ahead with the weariness of a questing hawk. It occurred to him that Carmody might be forted up for an ambush — might try to get in another sneak shot like the one he'd triggered when his bronc reared up. But the menace of ambush didn't cause Fayette to slow his pace; he rimmed the hills without halting and was halfway down the wooded west slope when he saw a meadow's grey-green sprawl below him.

It was only a glimpse through an opening in the timber, gained as his bronc slid down a steep bank. But in that brief moment two details of the scene registered sharply in Fayette's mind. There was grass in the meadow, and he'd seen cows down there. But the cows weren't grazing; they'd stood with their heads held high — *as if watching something!*

That meant just one thing to Jim Fayette. It meant that Kid Carmody was close ahead. Not more than a mile at most

Perhaps less. Fayette cocked the Winchester and rode with it cradled across his left arm, ready for instant use. Harlequin's pock-marked renegade had outsmarted him once today, but this was going to be different.

Or so he thought.

Chapter VIII

It was a matter of minutes until Fayette reached the clearing and saw Kid Carmody halfway across the meadow. The Bootjack rider was frantically flogging his wounded bronc, and even as Fayette raised his rifle, the floundering brute went down in a sprawling, lifeless heap.

Fayette halted his horse. He saw Carmody crawl hastily behind the dead bronc — and caught the flash of sunlight on gunmetal. Fayette grinned, and taking deliberate aim, triggered two shots in fast succession. Carmody fired at almost the same time, the flat report of his gun trailing the whine of a slug that was wide by several feet.

Fayette grinned again, and took stock of the situation. There was no need for hurry now. He built a cigarette and eased back in the saddle, taking a long look around. This meadow was at least five miles east of Spanish Canyon and six or seven miles from Chavez Corral. Unless the Bootjack contingent over there had riders cruising the hills, they wouldn't hear these shots. And even if they did, Carmody would be dead before they got here.

Leisurely, in the casual fashion of a man circling a spooky steer, Fayette rode a diagonal course across the meadow. The Kid fired again and again, but Fayette was a moving target and the distance was too great for accurate shooting. Only one of those slugs came close, and that one cut grass a yard behind Fayette's bronc.

Then, as Fayette neared a point that would put him in direct line with the bronc's carcass and thus deprive Carmody of his scant shelter, the Bootjack renegade jumped up with both hands held shoulder-high.

Whereupon Fayette chuckled, and keeping a wary watch, rode slowly up to the Kid. When he was close enough to see Carmody's amber eyes, he called, "Shuck that gungear, you stinking sneak!"

Kid Carmody obeyed at once, unbuckling his belt and letting it drop to the ground. There was a sullen scowl on his pock-pitted face and a malignant glint in his shifty eyes. Though he went by the name of "Kid," he was well past thirty, and there was a look of old, ingrained wickedness in his face.

"You won't git away with that Calico Creek job," he declared in a high-pitched, nasal voice. "You'll stretch rope for it, and so will your bushwhackin' partners."

"Mebbeso," Fayette muttered, and motioned for Carmody to proceed him back across the meadow.

"You aimin' to make me walk it?" the Kid demanded. Fayette nodded. "Get a move on, before I give you your needings here and now," he growled, and leaned down to slide the Winchester into his boot.

He was like that, bent over with both hands busy, when the Kid slipped a knife from his sleeve, lunged and stabbed with the flicking swiftness of a striking snake!

Fayette had no chance to parry that thrust. Even as he snatched his six gun from its holster, the blade hit him in the chest with terrific force. He was aware of its point in his flesh at the same instant his gun exploded.

Carmody loosed a gusty grunt, and when Fayette fired again, the Bootjack rider fell backward with a bug-eyed stare. Fayette watched him go down. He saw that the knife was no longer in Carmody's hand, and had the sickening sensation that the blade was still sticking in his chest, so firmly embedded that it would have to be yanked out. The very thought of it made him sick to his stomach. Then he looked down — and saw something that made his astonished stare match the Kid's bug-eyed expression of amazement.

The knife was dangling as if suspended by its point being caught in the leather of his riding jacket.

Suddenly Jim Fayette remembered the good-luck charm he'd bought from Pancho — the silver trinket he'd almost thrown away that night in Reservation. He had slipped it into the pocket of this riding jacket and forgotten all about it. But now he knew instantly what had happened. The blade's point had penetrated the soft silver just enough to nick his flesh.

Fayette disengaged the blade, seeing the blood on its sharp point and flinching at the thought of what this knife would have done to him except for the protection of Pancho's "spashal" charm. The Mexican urchin hadn't exaggerated its value; the good-luck trinket had meant the difference between life and death.

Fayette thought Carmody was dead, for both his slugs had hit the Kid in the chest, one of them cutting the corner of his shirt pocket. And Fayette was feeling a familiar nausea that he always felt after he'd killed a man at close range in a conflict for survival. Even though this man had pulled two sneak attempts against him, Fayette took no satisfaction in seeing him dead. He was turning his bronc to ride away when the Kid called whiningly, "Don't go — and leave me — to die alone."

That halted Fayette at once. He dismounted, and taking his canteen from the saddle, knelt beside Carmody. The Kid's eyes were glazing already, and his face had the peculiar waxen pallor of all dying men. He tried to take a drink, but he choked and the water was red with blood when it dribbled down his chin.

"This — makes us even," he rasped, a crooked grin creasing his chalky, pock-pitted face. "I got Dobie Dan — and you got me."

That death-doomed confession shocked Fayette completely. So his hunch had been right! Even though he'd guessed wrong about Breed Santana, it had been a Boot-jack knife that slaughtered Dan Pardee!

The canteen slid from Fayette's fingers and he felt an overwhelming desire to clutch Carmody's throat — to choke the last breath of life from this miserable son who'd murdered Dobie Dan.

But he fought that desire down, and

asked, "How did Harlequin find out about the right-of-way deed?"

"Are you — stayin' with me till I croak?" Carmody asked.

Fayette nodded, the strangeness of this bargain lost in the welter of hate that clutched him.

"Never did like to ride alone," Carmody mumbled, and grinned grotesquely.

"How about the deed?" Fayette demanded. "How'd Harlequin know Dan had it?"

"Sheriff Frobisher — told him. Jube heard —"

Blood rose in Carmody's throat then and he couldn't complete his report. But he'd said enough to make Jim Fayette remember the flimsy link that had evaded him in Reservation — the remote impression that had seemed vaguely significant that afternoon when Sheriff Frobisher had walked down the hotel hallway without making any noise. Frobisher, he knew now, had been eavesdropping in the hallway when Dobie Dan talked about the title which Fonso Chavez had "ciphered out, purty as you please."

Frobisher was the Judas responsible for Dan's death — as guilty as Shad Harlequin who'd ordered it, or this dying renegade who'd wielded the knife. Frobisher would pay, and so would Harlequin, as Carmody was paying now. But the first installment of that pay-off would be the chore Dan had wanted done — the breaking of Boot-jack's blockade!

There was no pity in Jim Fayette's smoke-blue eyes as he watched blood slobber from Carmody's lips. The wounded gunhawk went into a long spasm of wheezy coughing. When it ended, Kid Carmody was dead.

Chapter IX

For seven hours, while occasional puffs of powder smoke blossomed briefly on the rim of the ridge, Shad Harlequin raged and roared in the Calico Creek cabin. He cursed Kid Carmody, who'd failed to give warning of the dawn attack. He cursed Red Bastable for posting only one guard, and Breed Santana, who'd reported at dusk last night that the BD beef herd was at least two days down the trail.

"Fayette probably pulled this same trick at Chavez Corral," Harlequin fumed, "and shoved his herd through Spanish Canyon without a single shot being fired."

Breed Santana turned from a loophole in the logs. "The beef ees not reached Apache Flats yet," he insisted. "Steers do not have the weengs. They do not fly."

"Then what in hell did Fayette pull this stunt for?" Harlequin demanded, his hawk-beaked face black with anger.

Santana shrugged. *"Quien sabe?"* he murmured.

There were six other men in this smoke-filled room, and eight more behind the cabin. Three of them were bunked down with wounds and two were dead. But even then Bootjack had its attackers outnumbered more than five to one, and that fact was like a thorn in the thin skin of Shad Harlequin's pride.

Walking to a barricaded window, he peered through a small opening and said, "Only two guns up there now — just two damned guns holding us here like rats in a trap!"

"But them two has us hogtied same as if we was surrounded," Red Bastable grumbled. "They cover the whole clearing."

Harlequin glared at his redheaded foreman with a malignant glint in his piercing black eyes. "What kind of a stinking outfit is this?" he snarled. "I been handing out high wages to you galoots for months — fighting wages. Now, when the showdown comes, I got no fighters. Just a bunch of Gentle Annies afraid to risk their skins!"

One of the wounded men in the bunks uttered a groaning curse, and out back a rider hummed a stanza of *Hell among the Yearlings* with sardonic humour.

"If just one man could sneak back into the brush, he could circle around behind them polecats up there and break this thing loose," Harlequin muttered.

Breed Santana stepped over to the table for fresh shells. "Ees not far to the brush," he announced, his teeth flashing whitely in a grin. "But eet would be *jornado del muerte* — maybe."

"What the hell d'you mean, journey of death *maybe?*" Red Bastable demanded. He pointed a thick finger towards a shapeless form out in the sunlit yard and said: "Slats Gregg tried it, didn't he? And him so thin he'd have to stand twice in the same place to cast a shadow. But they sliced him down deader'n hell, and no maybe about it!"

The scar-faced Mexican shrugged. He reloaded his rifle with methodical skill and said: "Slats ees have bad luck because he ran fast. Per'aps if he crawl slow, like lazy snake, he weel not 'ave died — maybe."

Bastable snorted, but Shad Harlequin asked, "Think you could reach the brush, Breed?"

"*Quien sabe?*" Santana mused. "Who can say for sure? But I weel try — for one 'undred dollars."

"Hell, you've made a deal!" the Bootjack boss exclaimed.

He seldom smiled, but his thin lips twisted into something very close to a smile now. "Go ahead, Breed — and good luck!"

Santana held out a swarthy hand. "The *dinero?*" he suggested.

"What the hell! Don't you trust Shad to pay off?" Bastable scoffed.

"*Si,*" Santana said quietly. "I trust heem to pay off now."

Harlequin scowled, dug out his wallet and cautiously counted out the hundred dollars. "A lot of money for a few minutes' work," he muttered, handing it over with the hesitant manner of a miser.

Santana pocketed the bills and went through the rear window. Bastable said slyly, "You'll be taking it back from his dead body unless I miss my guess."

"Shouldn't be surprised," Harlequin agreed, and watched Santana start crawling across the yard, slowly — like a lazy snake.

It was almost sundown when Jim Fayette got back to the ridge above Calico Creek. So weak from loss of blood that dismounting seemed like a tremendous chore, he tied his horse back in the trees and was limping towards the rim when he saw something that stopped him in his tracks. Breed Santana and Single-O Smith were

hunkered behind the same rock outcrop —
shoulder to shoulder!

For an instant Fayette thought his eyes
had tricked him, that the pulsing pain in
his wounded leg had affected his reason.
This must be a witless, feverish dream.

But in the next moment Gus Odegarde
saw him and called, "We done got us another hired hand."

That didn't make sense to Fayette either,
until Gus explained how Santana had
sneaked up here and was on the verge of
shooting Single-O when he'd recognized
Smith as an old friend.

Santana nodded agreement. *"Mucho
amigo,"* he said grinningly.

And Smith drawled: "Me and Breed
rode together in Texas a long time ago. We
was what you call boozin' companions, eh,
Breed?"

Then the big outlaw glanced at Fayette's
blood-soaked leg and exclaimed, "Hell,
Jim, you're bleedin' like a jug'lared bull!"

Afterwards when Smith had bandaged
the wound and tied a tourniquet above it,
he said: "That's just a temporary job, Jim.
You'll have to ride into town and have a
sawbones fix it or you'll wind up one-
legged sure as hell."

"I'll ride into Reservation after I take a

looksee at Apache Flats," Fayette said stubbornly. "Not before."

Breed and Odegarde were back at the rim now, firing occasionally. It would be dark in another hour, Fayette estimated, and time to go. For there'd be no way of keeping Bootjack corralled at the cabin after that — and no need for it.

"How about Santana?" he asked. "You figger we can trust him, Single-O?"

"Hell, yes," Smith declared confidently. "Breed ain't no saint, for a fact. But I saved his hide once, and according to his code, that makes us brothers — *relatavos* — for life. He would swim through a river of manure with his mouth wide open, for me."

Fayette grinned and said: "We can sure use another gun. Will your bronc carry double?"

"If he won't, me and Breed will carry him," Single-O promised.

So it was that when dusk deepened into darkness, four men rode three horses toward Apache Flats. Behind them, at Calico Creek Camp, Shad Harlequin cursed his crew into hurried saddling and Red Bastable muttered, "I wonder what in hell happened to Breed."

During the next few hours, news of the

Calico Creek battle spread rapidly across the range. By midnight dead and wounded Bootjack riders had been brought to Reservation; Harlequin gunhawks roamed the hills in quest of their attackers, and Sheriff Frobisher tried to organize a posse to take the trail at daybreak.

"Jim Fayette has gone kill-crazy!" the big badge-toter declared. "Him and his Border riffraff are fixin' to take over this whole range — and they'll do it unless we help Shad Harlequin fight 'em down!"

Wild stories ran rampant, the reports being exaggerated with each telling. When the news reached Spur headquarters, the Calico Creek fight had become a wholesale massacre, with Fayette's raiders numbering upwards of fifteen men who'd swooped down on the camp at daybreak and ruthlessly slaughtered sleeping Bootjack riders in their bedrolls.

"A ghastly thing," Branch Shannon muttered upon hearing the report. He glanced at the old Gatling gun standing in the fireplace corner with other dust-covered relics of the days when he and Dan Pardee had defended this house against Apaches. "Fayette," he said, "has reverted to his renegade ways. I wouldn't be surprised if his outlaw bunch started raiding Spur before this thing is over."

"I don't believe it!" Gail exclaimed. "And I don't believe Jim would murder sleeping men!"

But there were tears in her eyes when she went to her room and finished packing the small trunk she was taking to El Paso. She couldn't forget how Jim had looked when he said: "That's how I'm going to fight Harlequin. *Like a Rio renegade!*"

He'd always been a trifle wild, even when he was courting her. Nothing, she guessed, would ever tame him. It was his nature to be rash and reckless — always ready for a fight or a frolic. As Dan Pardee remarked one time after Jim had lost three months' pay playing poker at the Belladonna: "Jim never does things halfway. It's whole hog or nothin' — from here to who laid the chunk!"

Gail was thinking about that when Keith Fabian gave her a farewell kiss just before she boarded the eastbound stage in Reservation. "Write to me," he pleaded, plainly dreading her departure, now that he'd regained his old place in her affections.

And Branch Shannon said sternly: "Forget you ever knew Jim Fayette. He's no good, honey — and he never will be."

Belle Nelson stood on the upstairs gallery, watching this scene with tight clasped hands and knowing how surely she had lost Keith. "The darn fool!" she whispered. "The darn crazy fool!"

But she wasn't referring to Keith Fabian. She was denouncing Jim Fayette, who'd deliberately thrown away his chance for a happy marriage, and hers as well. It didn't matter to Belle that she'd always played second fiddle in Keith's affections. Half a loaf was better than none. Much, much better. But now, because Jim Fayette was a fighting fool, she had lost Keith completely.

Belle watched the stagecoach roll out of town, seeing Gail's white handkerchief flutter at the window and Keith's farewell salute. Then she went dejectedly back to the two drab rooms she shared with her medico father.

At sundown Jim Fayette halted his dust-peppered bronc at the cattle corrals south of Reservation. Here he waited, keeping a wary watch as evening shadows lengthened across the flats. The tourniquet above the wound on his right leg had stopped the bleeding and brought a wooden numbness that obliterated all sense of pain. But he'd lost a lot of blood, and the wound needed cauterizing against infection.

Fayette built a cigarette and smoked it while dusk veiled the shapes of Reservation's buildings. Lamplit windows made yellow squares against the deepening darkness, and presently a group of riders galloped out of town, passing close enough for Fayette to recognize Sheriff Frobisher's pompous voice, although the words were jumbled in the hoof-pound of running horses.

"Must've been four or five in that bunch," Fayette calculated aloud. "Which means fewer guns against me if I'm seen."

Then he rode into town at a walk, using a trash-littered alley that ran behind the long row of business establishments on Main Street. Dismounting behind the Palace Hotel, he limped up a rear stairway to the second floor and made his way to Doc Nelson's room.

He knocked, and waited, and knocked again. Then he opened the door. The room was dark. Fayette swore softly, struck a match and lit the bracket lamp above Nelson's desk. A half-filled bottle of Colonel's Monogram stood above the litter of smaller bottles and bandages and surgical instruments. Fayette took a long drink, limped over to Doc's bed and eased on to it. No telling when the medico would come

94

in. Doc, he guessed, had been busy the last couple of days — busier than all git out.

Fayette was on the verge of falling asleep when he heard footsteps coming along the hallway. Rousing instantly, he drew his gun. That might be someone going to another room — or it might be a Bootjack rider wanting medical attention. Then the door opened and Belle Nelson exclaimed, "Jim!"

She came quickly to the bed, her glance attracted to his bloodstained pant leg. "So you got shot," she said. "Well, it serves you right!"

Fayette grinned and shifted to a sitting position. "I didn't come for a lecture," he said. "Where's Doc?"

"At Bootjack, patching up the results of your raid," Belle informed him. "He'll probably be there all night — and be stinking drunk when he gets home."

Then she went on into an adjoining room and soon returned with a basin of hot water. "Roll up your pant leg," she ordered. "I haven't got a medical diploma but I know most of the tricks — thanks to my drunken father."

She was, Fayette reflected, a thoroughly disillusioned girl — and prettier than he'd noticed before. Her sleek black hair was drawn back with artful severity, accentu-ating her high cheekbones. Her sultry eyes and pouting lips were somehow more ap-pealing than the smiles she'd always shown him before. She examined the discoloured wound with an impersonal regard which lacked any show of sympathy, and said again, "It serves you right."

"Why?" Fayette asked, entirely puzzled.

"Because you've messed up my romance — along with your own," she said angrily.

But her fingers were gentle when she cleansed the wound, and presently, when she cauterized it, she said softly, "I'm sorry to hurt you so, Jim — honestly I am."

And when it was done, she kissed him.

Chapter X

Another dusk. The end of another day of tedious, pain-racked riding for Jim Fayette. But because this was the crisis — the acid test of all his desperate planning — he fought off the weariness that weighted his slumped shoulders.

Overtaking the herd of stolen Bootjack steers, he had helped his motley crew drive the decoy herd across Apache Flats to join Kane's northbound drive. All day, then, they'd relentlessly pushed the combined herd up the trail, keeping the Bootjack stuff in front and setting up a great banner of dust that could be seen for miles. Yet no attack came, and that fact was positive proof to Fayette that Harlequin would set his trap in Spanish Canyon — and spring it tonight.

Now, with evening shadows quilting the timbered hills ahead, Fayette hunkered on his heels at the chuck wagon fire and listened to the talk around him. Some of these men were eating their last meal. No matter how the game went tonight, this would be the last supper for a few ill-fated fighters. There'd be riderless broncs roaming in the dismal dawn — broncs with empty saddles.

As if sharing the same thought, Andy Kane said: "Eat hearty, boys. It might be a long time before you see a cook unravel his Dutch ovens again."

"Per'aps never — maybe," Breed Santana suggested.

"What pessimism!" English Joe chided.

He was a queer cuss, this Englishman. He had the manners of a gentleman and talked like a scholar, but he wore the tattered garb of a saddle tramp and was seldom entirely sober. Gazing idly into the fire's embers, he quoted a piece of poetry:

> O Solitude, if I must with thee dwell,
> Let it not be among the jumbled heap
> Of murky buildings; climb with me
> the steep —
> Nature's observatory — whence the dell,
> Its flowery slopes, its river's crystal
> swell —

Big Monk Rodenbaugh reared up and bellowed, "Hogwash!"

"I beg to differ," English Joe said meekly. "It's the *Sonnet to Solitude*, by Keats."

"It's still hogwash to me," the ape-faced rider declared, "and I want no more of it!"

Single-O Smith chuckled gleefully. "Between your poems and that Mira music box, you've got Monk so mystified he can't sleep nights for wonderin' what it's all about," Smith said.

When the meal was finished, Fayette gave Kane his final instructions, telling him to go through Hoot Owl Hollow and stay clear of the Grant Trail all the way to Reservation.

"You figgerin' to ketch up with us before we git to town?" Kane asked, plainly worried, now that the time had come to test Jim's blockade-running plan.

"Yeah," Fayette said. "But if I don't, you've got my bill of sale in your pocket. Take what you can get for the steers, give the crew fighting wages — and use what's left to fight Bootjack. That's what Dobie Dan would've done."

Then, as he limped over to his horse, he added, "If you see young Pancho Garcia, give him a ten-dollar gold piece for luck."

Whereupon Fayette climbed clumsily into the saddle, suppressing a groan as the blood-gummed bandage pulled loose from his wound. And presently, as he rode out to the point of the decoy herd with Gus

Odegarde, the melancholy music of English Joe's Mira drifted across the dark — *La Paloma*'s haunting strains, soft and slow, as Gail had played it that night at Spur.

The thought that he'd never hear Gail play that tune again, nor any tune, stirred up a sense of futility. What the hell was the use of living if a man couldn't have the girl of his choice? Even if he succeeded in smashing Bootjack, it would be a hollow victory unless Gail was there to share it. Recalling Belle Nelson's words in town, Fayette cursed softly. He'd done a thorough job of messing up her romance along with his own. And even though her lips had caressed him with the warmth of a passionate and generous woman wanting affection, he knew that Keith Fabian was the man she really loved, and always would.

Fayette was thinking about that as the drive started up the trail toward Spanish Canyon. But later, when dusk's lavender shadows had deepened into mealy darkness and the brooding silence was broken only by a monotonous shuffle of hoofs, he had to fight off fuzzy layers of fatigue that made staying awake a tremendous chore. Then, for what seemed an endless interval, he thought about nothing at all — until finally Gus Odegarde called across the herd, "Spanish Canyon just ahead."

Even that didn't entirely arouse Fayette from his deep well of weariness. But it stirred a strand of impatience in him — an eagerness to get this grisly job done. For although his hope of breaking the blockade hinged entirely on this strategy, he hated the wanton slaughter it would bring. He was visualizing it, and dreading it, when the first shot came.

For a hushed instant, a rifle's report ran raggedly back between the high walls. Then, as guns blasted on both sides of the pass, hell broke loose in Spanish Canyon.

In this first moment, as muzzle flame ripped the moonless gloom and a roar of reverberating sound filled the canyon, Fayette's mind registered the fact that Shad Harlequin must have brought his whole crew for a wipeout massacre here tonight. More than twenty guns were blasting from vantage points all along the Canyon. Bawling steers lunged frantically, trying to turn back but being pushed onward by the press of hard-driven brutes behind them. Lead laced the air like wind-whipped sleet; slugs whined so close to Fayette that he heard a bullet's meaty *plop* as it dropped a steer at his stirrup.

"Keep 'em coming!" he yelled, his voice lost in the wild bedlam of exploding guns and the clatter of hoofs and horns as he lashed confused cattle forward with a rope end.

On the opposite side of the trail, Gus Odegarde also swung his rope, and cursed the cattle in a croaking, dust-choked voice. Single-O Smith and Breed Santana were close up now, with English Joe and Monk Rodenbaugh behind them, all desperately flanking the steers. Then came Alabam Bell, Tod Foyle and Charlie Moss, using their guns to frighten the drag forward.

When dead steers had piled up so high that their bodies built a barrier across the canyon, Fayette and Odegarde dropped back to new positions. Riders retreated all along the line as the slaughter continued for what seemed an eternity to Jim Fayette, until at last the crew was fanned out behind the drag end of the herd and there was no more driving to do.

Then he tallied his riders, knowing that some would be missing. Alabam Bell and Charlie Moss failed to show. "Heard Charlie scream," Tod Foyle reported excitedly. "He must of been shot out of his saddle and then got trampled to death."

A wounded steer charged blindly from the canyon, its horn grazing Fayette's injured leg. The pain of that turned him sick to his stomach, but it didn't spoil his aim, for he dropped the enraged brute just as it lunged into the scattering riders.

"Now," he said grimly, "we give those Bootjack sons some lead. Spread out and keep moving while you dab it to 'em!"

Chapter XI

Breeze-blown streamers of dust rose above the cattle corrals at the south end of Reservation; they drifted across Main Street and settled finally against the barren slope of Cemetery Hill. There was a pattern of premonition in the dust's journey, but Branch Shannon didn't see it.

This was at noon, and Shannon sat with Keith Fabian on the Palace Hotel veranda listening to Jock Gilligan, who'd just come across from the Blue Bull Saloon.

"Harlequin is in there celebratin' with Bastable and Sheriff Frobisher," the liveryman reported excitedly. "Shad says Fayette kept pushin' beef into Spanish Canyon last night like a madman; says there was only three or four Fayette riders left when Shad and Red came away from the canyon a little before daylight. I reckon Jim is licked all to hell. Even if he got out of it alive, them Bootjack gunhawks will hunt him down. Shad told 'em not to come back without Fayette — dead or alive!"

Shannon lit a fresh cigar, his fingers not

quite steady. "Jim was doomed the day he decided to fight Harlequin," he muttered in a regretful tone of voice. "I tried to tell him that, but Jim wouldn't listen. He went loco the night Dan Pardee was murdered, and he'll never get over it."

Which was when Shad Harlequin, flanked by Bastable and Frobisher, came swaggering along the sidewalk with whisky courage glinting in their eyes.

"If Harlequin asks about that railroad beef contract, tell him you're not going to bid on it," Keith Fabian said urgently to Shannon.

"Why should I?" Spur's boss demanded.

The yellow-haired young banker looked embarrassed. "Bootjack is the only big depositor I've got left," he admitted. "I — well, Branch, I can't give you the cash you'd need for a forfeit bond."

"But I've got that contract!" Shannon exclaimed. "If you can't make me the loan, I'll get it somewhere else!"

Almost at once then, Shad Harlequin called arrogantly: "I busted the outlaw half of Spur last night. Now I'll buy the other half, Shannon — if the price is right."

The brazen confidence of that declaration shocked Branch Shannon. He glanced at Sheriff Frobisher and saw how openly this grafting lawdog was backing Boot-jack's rapacious owner.

"Well?" Harlequin asked. "What's your price?"

Shannon's age-mottled face went pale, and there was a dismal tone of foreboding in his voice when he said, "It's not for sale."

"It will be!" Harlequin shouted brashly. "It'll be for sale cheap one of these days!"

He made a sweeping gesture with his hand. "It'll all be Bootjack range!" he announced, and smacked his thin lips. "Tonto, Spanish Grant, Border Desert — the whole damned outfit!"

Red Bastable peered at Shannon and asked, "You wasn't figgerin' to bid on that railroad contract, was you, Shannon?"

"What business is it of yours?" Spur's owner asked angrily.

Bastable glanced at his boss, grinned and said: "He thinks we're funnin', Shad. He don't believe we got this country in our vest pocket."

Sheriff Frobisher loosed a hoot of drunken laughter and Harlequin pointed a finger at Keith Fabian. "You better tell your friend Shannon to stay clear of that beef contract. If he should outbid me, any paper you're holdin' against Spur won't be worth a plugged peso. Keep that in mind, Fabian!"

When Harlequin had swaggered back to the Blue Bull with his two grinning companions, Jock Gilligan muttered: "I guess Jim Fayette wasn't so loco after all. He said Harlequin was goin' to grab everythin' in sight if he wasn't stopped."

"Harlequin can't crowd me off Spur!" Shannon exclaimed. "We've got laws to protect range rights in this country!"

"The same laws we had when Bootjack pushed them Spanish Grant outfits off their range," Gilligan reminded him slyly.

"Shad was drunk," Keith Fabian muttered. "He was spouting whisky talk. But I wouldn't outbid him, Branch. That might force a fight you couldn't win."

"I've got to have that contract," Shannon said stubbornly.

Then he saw Jim Fayette — saw him come riding along Main Street like a slumped, saddle-beat old man.

"Jim!" he exclaimed, and rushed down the steps to meet him.

But Fayette didn't dismount. And he didn't seem to see Shannon at all. There was no smile of recognition on his haggard, beard-bristled face. He halted his sweat-stained bronc and peered at Jock Gilligan through bleak, red-rimmed eyes and asked, "Any cattle buyers in town?"

Gilligan gulped. He nodded his head. "Couple over at the Belladonna a few minutes ago," he said.

"Why do you ask?" Shannon called.

Fayette jerked a thumb towards the cattle pens at the south end of town. "Just drove five hundred head of BD steers into the corrals," he drawled. "They're a trifle shrunk up — but they'll make fair beef."

Whereupon he rode over to the Belladonna and, dismounting stiffly, limped inside like a man not quite drunk and not quite sober.

"You reckon he's gone plumb crazy?" Gilligan demanded, staring at Shannon. "Harlequin said —"

Then they heard it. A familiar, plaintive sound that was unmistakable to any man, woman or child in the cow country. The bawling of corralled cattle!

"My stars!" Keith Fabian exclaimed.

And Gilligan blurted: "He's done it, Branch! He's brought a beef herd through, just like he said he'd do."

But Shannon wasn't listening. He was watching two men across Main Street — seeing Red Bastable and Sheriff Frobisher tromp towards the Belladonna with guns in their hands, watching them take up positions on either side of the saloon doorway. And he knew that Jim Fayette wouldn't survive both those guns.

Poker Pat McGurk stared at Jim Fayette as if he saw a ghost. "The saints be praised!" he shouted, and reached for his private bottle. "Ye look six years older than Satan, lad — but it's glad I am to be buyin' ye a drink!"

"Where'd those cattle buyers go?" Fayette asked in the tone of a man fighting to stay on his feet.

"Over to the Chink's eatin'," McGurk said. "Have a jolt of panther juice, Jimmy boy."

"Not now," Fayette muttered. "Not till I've sold my steers and paid the boys their wages."

"But I thought —"

"Don't give a damn what anybody thought," Fayette rasped.

He limped back to the batwings and was stepping through them when he heard Branch Shannon's panic-stricken voice lance across the street: "Jim — go back!"

At this same instant, Fayette glimpsed the two waiting men and knew why Shannon had tried to warn him — and knew also that the warning had come too late. This, he understood, was the end of the trail in more ways than one — the end of the long and lonely trail an orphan kid had taken in Texas.

"Grab, you smart-alecky son," Bastable snarled, "before I give it to you cold-turkey!"

There was a hot brightness in Bastable's eyes — the metallic, unblinking brightness of a hungry buzzard scenting dead flesh.

Forcing calm confidence into his voice, Fayette drawled, "You're outnumbered, Bastable."

Astonishment bagged Bastable's eyes. "What the hell d'you mean — outnumbered?"

"We got you two to one, ain't we?" Sheriff Frobisher sneered.

"Sure," Fayette admitted, a thin, sardonic grin twisting his bloodless lips. "But the whole BD crew is down at the stock pens right now — and a few besides. Men like Single-O Smith and Monk Rodenbaugh and Faro Pratt."

Then he said: "Listen, Bastable. Listen to them beef steers bawlin'."

"Hell — we butchered all your beef in Spanish Canyon last night!" Red Bastable scoffed.

"You butchered two hundred head of cattle," Fayette said quietly, not shifting his gaze from Bastable's gun. "But they weren't mine."

"Then whose in hell were they?" the Bootjack foreman demanded.

"Harlequin's," Fayette drawled, a ghost of his old devil-be-damned grin creasing his gaunt face. "My herd came up through Hoot Owl Hollow while your butcher boys were slaughtering Bootjack stuff rustled out of the Fandango Hills the day we kept you corralled at Calico Creek."

The astonishing realization that this was true — that his boss had been tricked into the very trap he'd set — struck Red Bastable with an impact that shook him visibly. In this moment of monstrous consternation, his glance shifted to Sheriff Frobisher. Which was the chance for survival, but just time enough to pay another installment for Dan Pardee's ruthless murder.

Instantly marshalling all the skill the renegade years had given him, Fayette drew his gun. And vividly remembering Kid Carmody's confession, he chose his target without hesitation, slamming a slug at Jube Frobisher. The lawdog fired at the same instant, his bullet grazing Fayette's ribs

111

with a force that knocked the wind out of him.

The rest of it was a smoke-hazed hell of confusion to Jim Fayette. He fired a second slug at Frobisher's floundering shape, saw the sheriff go down and heard his elbows strike the stoop boards. Then, as the muscles of Fayette's back flinched against the expected smash of Red Bastable's bullet, he whirled to face the Bootjack foreman.

Which was when he glimpsed Poker Pat McGurk standing between the saloon batwings with a short-barreled scattergun aimed at Bastable's belt buckle. "If ye so much as blink an eye, I'll blow ye to smithereens!" the old Irishman warned.

Jim Fayette took a deep breath and grinned. His side was bleeding, but he guessed the bullet had merely slashed the skin above his ribs. He said, "Thanks, Pat."

Then he stepped over to Bastable. "Drop that gun!" he ordered, a savage eagerness riding his voice. And when the redhead obeyed, Fayette sheathed his own weapon.

The BD crew, attracted by the shooting, galloped in from the cattle pens and rode through the crowd that jammed Belladonna Alley.

"What's up?" Andy Kane demanded,

staring at Frobisher's sprawled body.

"Just paying off a couple of debts for Dobie Dan," Fayette announced.

Then he snapped a vicious right to Bastable's bloody face.

"What the hell!" Red yelped.

He dodged against the saloon wall, blood spurting from his nose.

Lunging in close, Fayette targeted Bastable's face and felt a flaring exultation when his blood-smeared knuckles bashed Red's nose again. He pounded Bastable's belly with both fists, and heard Jock Gilligan yell, "Smash him down, lad — smash the spalpeen down!"

Bastable had no relish for this fight. His whisky courage had faded at the sight of McGurk's scattergun; now he kept dodging, all his efforts defensive. He tried to ward off Fayette's two-fisted barrage of blows. He wheeled and floundered, endeavouring to save his bloody face from further punishment.

"Fight — you stinking son!" Fayette snarled, and punctuated that command with a sledging smash that knocked Bastable's head against the saloon wall.

The Bootjack ramrod slumped sideways as if stunned. His slack-jawed mouth hung open and a blank, unseeing stare came into his eyes. He would have fallen then except that Fayette reached out and steadied him.

Shad Harlequin had watched this one-sided contest from the rear fringe of the crowd. Now he turned and strode unsteadily toward the Blue Bull Saloon. He heard the meaty impact of Fayette's fist against his foreman's face, that sound soon followed by Jock Gilligan's voice crackling: "Ye downed him, lad! He's out cold!"

Whereupon Harlequin cursed, and entering the Blue Bull, poured himself a drink at the deserted bar. For the first time in years, he was alone in this town. Jube Frobisher was dead, Bastable had allowed himself to be battered unconscious — and Reservation was full of BD riders. It made a man's guts crawl to be so damned alone.

Harlequin scowled at his reflection in the back-bar mirror. And in this moment he saw himself the victim of one man — saw how completely Jim Fayette had out-maneuvered him. Not only had Fayette broken the blockade and brought a beef herd to town; he'd tricked Bootjack into slaughtering a big bunch of its own steers. In three days' time the whole picture had changed. Instead of being blockaded into bankruptcy, Jim Fayette was now cock of the roost in Reservation.

"Damn his hide!" Harlequin exclaimed. "I should've had his throat cut along with Pardee!"

During the next four days, Border Desert riders tromped the plank sidewalks of Reservation like a hilarious horde of battle-scarred troopers on a spree. And so they were. Even Jim Fayette took on more than his usual amount of whisky and played poker with more luck than he'd ever had before. Harlequin and Bastable had ridden out of town as soon as Red could climb groggily into the saddle, and no Bootjack rider had appeared at the sheriff's burial.

Then, on the morning of the fifth day, when bedrolls were being loaded into the BD chuck wagon in preparation for the trip south, Belle Nelson came running down to the stock pens and announced: "Branch Shannon has been shot! Spur's Chinese cook just came after Dad — said there was a big fight last night and Branch is hurt bad!"

Fayette loosed a curse. No wonder there'd been no Harlequin men around town. They'd been busy raiding Spur. And they'd done it while he was carousing here in town. That somehow made it seem worse; as if his careless celebrating had contributed to Spur's downfall.

"Guess BD will be next on their list," Andy Kane prophesied. "We'd best git a wiggle on us, Jim — or we might find nothin' but ashes and slaughtered stock when we git there."

Which was, Fayette knew, a reasonable prediction. Smarting under his defeat at Spanish Canyon, Harlequin would want revenge, and he'd lose no time trying to get it. Spur had been first, being the closest to Bootjack; but Border Desert would be next. No doubt about it.

"How many men did Spur lose last night?" Fayette asked Belle.

"The cook didn't say," she reported. "He just said it was a big fight — and he thought Shannon was dying."

Whereupon Fayette remembered how Branch had tried to warn him in the saloon doorway five days before — how he'd said afterwards: "I was wrong, Jim. I guess there's only one way to beat Bootjack — the way you and Dan tried to tell me."

Branch had been too proud to ask for help, and because Keith Fabian was with him at the time, Jim hadn't offered it. Afterwards he'd got drunk and forgotten all about it. Now Gail's father wounded — perhaps dying. And she was away at school.

The crew were all a-saddle now, waiting for him. "You about ready to hit a shuck for home?" Andy Kane asked.

"I'm not going," Fayette said, eyeing the grouped riders. "Reckon I'll take a few boys and give Branch a hand if he needs it."

"Hell, no!" Gus Odegarde objected. "Shannon wouldn't help us save our homes when we asked him to. Now let him fry in his own fat!"

"I didn't ask you to come with me," Fayette snapped. Then he turned to Kane and said: "I'll take Single-O's boys with me. You and the rest hightail for Border Desert, and I hope you get there in time."

Andy Kane sat in frowning silence for a moment. He opened his mouth to speak, changed his mind and turned his horse towards home without a word. Which was, Fayette understood, Andy's way of showing how he felt about splitting BD's forces at a time like this.

Grimly, as a man caught between conflicting loyalties, Fayette watched Kane's crew ride off. Those men were his real friends — the only friends he had left. They'd do anything in their power to save Dobie Dan's old ranch. But they'd be outnumbered and might lose by the margin of men he was taking to Spur.

Shrugging off that futile realization, Fayette turned to the riders who remained. There was no friendship here — just a hard-case crew fighting for gun wages. With the possible exception of English Joe, they'd as soon shoot a man as look at him. "Scum of the Border," Branch Shannon had called them. Yet now they might be all that stood between Spur and Shad Harlequin's rapacious dream of conquest.

"How about one more drink before we leave town?" Single-O suggested.

Whereupon Fayette grinned mirthlessly. "Yeah," he muttered. "One more drink — then a lot more shooting."

Chapter XII

Gail Shannon sat alone in the rumbling, dust-hazed stagecoach. She wore a little black hat tilted pertly on her blonde hair, and there was no sign of fear in her brown eyes. But Gail was afraid — more afraid than she'd ever been.

The swaying Concord clattered down a stone-studded ridge and started across the parched flats east of Reservation. The four-horse hitch stirred dust into a back-drifting billow, against which Gail lowered the canvas window flaps. And remembering that she'd done this same thing on the eastward trip, she felt a sharp sense of nostalgia. Three weeks wasn't a long time to be away from home, not long enough to make her forget the counsel of a kindly old cowman who'd said, "Don't you worry about anything." But she couldn't help worrying. Apprehension and uncertainty had clawed at her courage all the weary miles from El Paso, increasing each day until fear was like a cold hand clutching at her heart.

Keith Fabian's message had been brutally brief: "Come home at once. Branch hurt."

That had been bad enough — so bad she'd taken the next train west. But in Tombstone, where she'd changed to this stage, she had seen a piece in the *Weekly Epitaph* which referred to Branch Shannon as the instigator of a bloody range war: "Siding with Jim Fayette, who turned Border Desert into a renegades' roost for wanted criminals, Branch Shannon has brought death and destruction to the formerly peaceful country around Reservation. This once respected cattle king is now a veritable fugitive from the forces of law and order which are closing in on him from all sides."

The newspaper's startling report had astonished Gail, even though she knew it must have been garbled. Her father had denounced Jim Fayette; he'd even had a notice printed in the *Epitaph* to that effect. Yet now the paper said he'd joined Jim's crazy fight — that Branch Shannon was in partnership with the very men he'd called Border scum.

Even the grouchy old stage driver seemed to share the newspaper's hostile attitude. "You won't find no welcome-home

committee waitin' for you in Reservation,"
he'd informed her. "Folks ain't likin' all
the gunsmoke that's driftin' out of the
Fandango Hills."

But Keith would be there to welcome
her and explain what this was all about —
loyal, handsome Keith, who had ignored
the smiles of every girl in Reservation, including that dusky-haired flirt, Belle
Nelson.

Gail was thinking about that when the
stage halted so abruptly that she lurched
forward from the seat. Then a voice called,
"You got a lady passenger?" — a voice that
sounded familiar.

The driver said, "Yes," and when Gail
opened the door, she saw Jim Fayette
standing between two saddled horses. He
didn't say anything for a moment. He gave
her a deliberate, almost lingering appraisal;
then he touched the brim of his dust-
peppered hat with casual courtesy and
said, "You're to come with me, Gail."

"Why?" she asked, entirely puzzled.

"Your father's orders."

Then she noticed the shoulder brands
on the broncs behind him and felt something close to utter bewilderment. "What
are you doing with Spur horses?" she demanded.

"I'm Spur's new foreman," he announced, not smiling, even around the eyes, where he'd always smiled when he was funning.

"What happened to Ike Ogden?" Gail demanded.

"He died," Fayette said.

While Gail was absorbing that startling news, the grouchy stage driver complained, "I ain't got all day."

Fayette glanced up at the driver, a brittle hardness in his eyes. "You've got whatever time it takes," he declared, and added, "See that Miss Shannon's baggage is put off at the Palace Hotel."

"But perhaps I don't choose to ride with you, Jim," Gail suggested, resenting his arrogant unsmiling ways.

"You'll ride with me, one way or another," he muttered, and motioned for the driver to depart.

A swift surge of rebellious anger rose in Gail. Just who did Jim Fayette think he was — handing out orders like a sphinx-faced slave driver? But something she saw in his unswerving eyes told her that he wasn't bluffing — that she'd have to ride with him, *one way or another.*

As the stage went on, she asked urgently, "How is Dad?"

Fayette ignored the question. He lifted a pair of brush-scarred chaps from one of the saddles and handed them to her. "Better figger a way to wear these," he said, "so the catclaw won't tear that pretty skirt to ribbons."

Whereupon he turned to the horses and gave his attention to tightening saddle cinches while Gail contrived a way of wearing the chaps. Jim Fayette, she reflected, had acquired a disagreeable habit of giving orders and ignoring questions.

"How badly is Dad hurt?" she demanded insistently. Fayette didn't look at her. He kept fiddling with his saddle gear, and in the long moment before he answered Gail braced herself. Branch, she guessed, must be hurt bad.

Then Fayette said flatly, "Your father is dead."

The shock of that was like a physical blow to Gail — like a terrific, paralyzing blow. For a long moment she didn't speak and she didn't move. She just stood there staring at Jim Fayette with wide, disbelieving eyes. Then all the fear of the past few days seemed to burst somewhere inside and a black wave of anguish surged through her. Yet even then, with the salty sting of unshed tears in her eyes and a lump in her throat that made her lips quiver, Gail Shannon didn't cry. She picked up the reins of the nearest horse and climbed into the saddle.

While they rode northwest across the flats, Gail fought down the forming sobs inside her. Branch had never liked crying women. He had even talked away her tears when her mother died seven years before. "She wouldn't want you crying like a calf with the colic," he'd said. "She's up there with the angels now, singing and smiling sweeter than any of them."

He had made it seem real, and beautiful. He'd even read to her about heaven from her mother's Bible. "People you love don't die," he had explained. "They just go on ahead and wait for you."

That reflection helped Gail to keep back the tears. But it didn't ease the ache in her throat, nor thaw the cold knot of grief inside her. Presently, when the horses began the steep climb into the hills, she asked, "What caused the trouble, Jim?"

"A beef contract to deliver one thousand prime steers to the railroad construction camp at Tonto Junction, on or before July first," he said.

"Did Dad outbid Harlequin?"

Fayette nodded, and told her about the

124

raid, and the new sheriff Harlequin had maneuvered into office to replace Frobisher. "One of his own riders — a quick-trigger galoot named Abe Drago."

"How many of Spur's old crew are left?" Gail asked.

But instead of answering that question, Fayette suddenly swerved his horse, spurring it against hers so violently that her bronc was forced down a steep bank. And at almost the same instant a rifle began blasting somewhere above them. Bullets plunked into the bank, whipping up spurts of dust where their horses had been only a few seconds before. A slug snapped off a catclaw branch so close to Gail's head that a sharp barb of the flying branch scratched her cheek.

Panic-stricken by the realization that the next bullet might hit her, Gail struggled to stay on her sliding, wildly-plunging horse. The frightened animal crashed through a mesquite thicket, the barbed branches ripping at Gail's sleeves as she tried to protect her face. Fayette was firing from somewhere behind her. She could hear his gun, but the scuffed-up dust was like sun-glinted fog and she couldn't see through it. In this moment of chaotic confusion, she felt utterly alone — abandoned. Stark terror gripped her and she had an overwhelming urge to scream.

But Fayette's voice cut through the gun blasts — through the snarl and whine of searching slugs. "Keep moving," he ordered, and crowded her horse deeper into the protecting arroyo.

His drawling voice showed no excitement, no fear. It was calmly reassuring and he rode up beside her, so that his tall body was like a living shield between her and the continuing gunshots.

In a little while, all sense of panic left Gail. Her hysterical dread disappeared entirely and she relaxed in her saddle. Thinking how near she had been to screaming, she felt ashamed — and then downright angry.

"Couldn't that fool see I was a woman?" she demanded.

"Wouldn't make much difference to a Bootjack rider," Fayette said.

Bullets still snarled through the brush. But they weren't close now, as the first few had been. And the sound of firing was more remote, the reports running along the deep arroyo like drifting echoes of a gun being fired a long way off.

Presently the shooting ceased altogether and Fayette said, "Now we wait — and listen."

For a few moments, while the round-about silence was broken only by the gusty breathing of their broncs, Gail sat watching her companion, seeing the way he sat poised in his saddle with his head canted to one side. There was the look of a hunting hawk in Jim's eyes as he scanned the upper reaches of the arroyo. Two old scars made small, pale tracks against the deep tan of his left cheek, and there was another scar on the bridge of his nose. His long lips, thinly compressed now with the intentness of his questing, had a cynical twist that she'd never noticed before. And he looked older and more haggard than she'd ever seen him.

She was wondering whether he still smiled in the same devil-be-damned way as she watched him dismount and pick up a rock.

"Mebbe we can fool him," Fayette muttered, hefting the missile. Then he threw it far up the arroyo. A faint crash drifted back, and he said, "It'll sound louder up above."

A moment later Gail heard the hoof-pound of a running horse somewhere on the ridge above them — and saw Jim's lips loosen into his familiar grin. It was brief, but it changed him completely, softening all the contours of his face and driving the brittle wariness out of his eyes. The two scars on his cheek were like twin dimples; his long lips had a puckered fullness and he looked ten years younger.

"That galoot thinks we're riding up the arroyo and he's gone to head us off," he said. "But we'll circle around him. Or at least we'll try to."

Afterwards, while they rode up the steep, brush-tangled slope, stopping at frequent intervals to look and listen, Gail asked again, "How many of the crew left?"

"Two," Fayette answered. "Pop Pettigrew and Banjo Jones."

That news added to the slogging sense of futility in Gail. Branch, Ike Ogden and all those other men dead! Spur being defended by a bunch of Border scum against Bootjack, which had the law on its side.

"Do you think there's a chance for Spur to make good on that beef contract now?" she asked finally.

"Not much," Fayette said, and eyed her thoughtfully. "But it's all the chance you've got of saving Spur, Gail. Your father posted a big forfeit that he would deliver the beef on time, and he mortgaged the ranch to do it. If the forfeit goes, Spur goes with it."

"I had no idea Dad was so short of cash!" Gail exclaimed. "We'd had a couple of real bad years, but I didn't know Spur was hit so hard that Dad couldn't put up a cash forfeit without borrowing money. Why — he shouldn't have sent me to school if things were that bad!"

"Branch wanted you to be a lady," Fayette said, almost scoffingly. Or so it seemed to Gail.

It was close to sundown when they topped the summit of Cathedral Divide. And here, as they crossed the boulder-strewn crest, Gail met Single-O Smith for the first time. The black patch over his eye gave Smith the ferocious look of a blood-thirsty pirate as he stood above the trail with a Winchester cradled in the crook of his arm. He acknowledged Fayette's intro-duction with a guttural grunt and then turned to his patient scanning of the sur-rounding slopes.

As Gail rode on across the crest with Fayette, she said frowningly, "Is that the kind of men Spur has on its pay-roll now?"

"Yeah — just a bunch of six-gun smokeroos, including your foreman."

Gail ignored his sarcasm and presently, when they reached the western rim of Ca-thedral Divide, she halted her horse and gazed out across the broad basin to where Spur's sun-glinted windmill stood like a silver sentinel above a big house — above barns and sheds and sprawling corrals.

Home. Even though the rambling, L-shaped house was too far away for her to see it distinctly, Gail knew exactly how it looked. There'd be the long front gallery with its weather-warped rawhide-bottom chairs behind the spur-scarred railing. Beside each window were iron shutters, rusty with age and showing the dents of Apache bullets fired before she was born. Inside, where a massive stone fireplace reached halfway across the rear wall of the living room, there'd be the solid mahogany furniture Branch had imported all the way from New Mexico; colorful hand-woven rugs from Old Mexico; and the huge leather lounge — "a bunk big enough for a man to spread out on," as her father had called it.

Her own room, with all its girlhood treasures, would be the same as she'd left it; Branch's room, cluttered with ledgers and tally books; the big kitchen where Chinee Charlie padded about in his Shanghai sandals. . . .

It held a host of memories, that old house. Seeing it now, Gail sat tight-lipped, trying to swallow the lump in her throat, holding back the tears that kept misting her eyes. If only Branch were waiting down there to welcome her, to shout, "Welcome home, honey!" And take her in his big arms! But Branch was gone, and it wouldn't seem like home without him. Nothing would seem the same.

Then the thought came to her that Spur was more than a home. It was a monument to Branch Shannon, who'd spent his life building it — to the proud old cowman who had died defending it. She glanced at Fayette and found him leisurely fashioning a cigarette. His face showed no expression at all, no awareness of what this homecoming meant to a grief-stricken girl. Gail wished it were Keith Fabian who was sitting there. Keith would be sympathetic and deeply concerned. He'd tell her to cry on his shoulder and he'd wipe away her tears with his handkerchief.

But even though Jim's casual indifference stirred a sense of resentment in Gail, she couldn't ignore the fact that he'd probably saved her life down there on the ridge trail. And his calm voice had kept her from screaming like a schoolgirl.

"We've got to save Spur," she said finally. "We've just got to."

That seemed to startle Fayette. He gave

her a speculative glance and asked, "You planning to fight it out with Shad Harlequin?"

"Of course," Gail said. "What else would you expect me to do?"

"Well, judging by what you told me the last time we met, I thought you'd shed a few tears and then move into town *muy pronto*. That's what most high-toned girls would do."

"What makes you think I'm so high-toned, Jim?"

He came near to smiling then. "Well, you sort of look that way. Or you did, before the brush scratched you all up."

It occurred to Gail that she must look a fright. She had lost her hat in that mad plunge down the bank, and her blouse was torn in three different places. Added to that were the catclaw scratch on her cheek and a liberal coating of dust.

This self-appraisal brought another swift sense of resentment against Jim Fayette. "Why," she asked arrogantly, "couldn't I have been met in town instead of being dragged through the brush like a law-dodging saddle-tramp?"

"Your dad's orders," Fayette reported, and then, as they rode slowly down the western slope of the divide, he explained why he'd spent the past three days meeting the Tombstone stage down there on the flats. "Just before Branch died, he asked me to bring you up here, direct. Said he wanted you to see Spur and hear how things stood before folks in town talked to you."

That banished Gail's anger. She asked, "Did — did he mention any names?"

Fayette nodded.

"Keith's?" Gail asked.

"Yeah," Fayette said slowly, as if disliking this part of his chore. "Branch said to tell you that Keith tried to talk him out of bucking Harlequin's bid and refused to lend him the money for the forfeit. That's why your dad wanted you to come here before you made up your mind."

"But why should Keith turn down a loan to Dad?" Gail demanded, completely puzzled.

Fayette shrugged. "Might have had any number of reasons. He might have used that way of trying to keep Branch from bidding, so's there wouldn't be trouble. Or maybe it was because Bootjack is the bank's big depositor. I never liked your yellow-haired boy friend, Gail, but I don't blame him for not lending Branch the money."

Gail smiled inwardly. Jim, she guessed, was trying to be gallant about Keith. Which was something new, for he had always shown his dislike. He'd once told her that he hated all bankers because a Texas bank had foreclosed a mortgage on his boyhood home after his folks had been killed in a wagon smashup. "They're a conniving, lily-fingered breed of rascals," he had declared. "I'd sooner trust a tinhorn gambler."

"Where did Dad borrow the money?" she inquired.

"From Pat McGurk. After the fighting started, Pat offered to sell the mortgage cheap."

"Why?" Gail asked.

"Well, a lot of folks seem to think Spur is done for, including Keith Fabian. They figger this'll all be Bootjack range when the shooting stops — which wouldn't make a mortgage very valuable."

It was dusk now, and Gail couldn't see Jim's face. But there was a taunting note in his voice, as if he were prodding her, deliberately rubbing salt in a raw wound. She was wondering about that when they rode into Spur's yard and she saw Belle Nelson standing in the lamplit doorway.

"What's she doing here?" Gail demanded.

"Helping Chinee Charlie take care of the wounded," Fayette said. "Doc Nelson has his hands full, with four or five gunshot cases at Bootjack besides the ones here. Belle has been a regular angel of mercy."

Angel of mercy! That brazen, man-chasing daughter of a drunken old medico!

Gail felt a senseless urge to laugh. What a homecoming this was! Her father dead, Spur poised on the ragged edge of ruin, and Belle Nelson standing in the doorway. The same Belle Nelson who'd used all her woman's wiles to win Keith Fabian away from her in the old days.

It was enough to make a girl laugh — or cry. But Gail did neither. She dismounted at the gallery and handed Jim her bronc's reins. Then she went up the steps and said, "It was nice of you to help, Belle."

The medico's daughter hurried out to meet her. "I'm so sorry for you!" she exclaimed throatily. "Let's have a good cry, Gail, and we'll both feel better."

Whereupon a faint smile curved Gail's lips and she said: "We Shannons don't cry, Belle. It's against the rules."

Chapter XIII

Jim Fayette stood for a moment watching the two girls go into the house. They made a contrasting pair, for Belle Nelson was a striking brunette and she wore a pink calico dress that seemed especially feminine beside Gail's torn blouse and dusty chaps.

He heard Chinee Charlie exclaim, "Come kitchen dlink coffee, Missy Gail, while Cholly ketchum supper!"

And when he led the broncs toward the horse corral, Monk Rodenbaugh called from the bunkhouse doorway, "Was that the queen from El Paso?"

"Yeah," Fayette muttered, resenting this brawny rider's reference to Gail.

"She didn't look like no fine lady to me," Monk declared. "She looked like a scrub from who hid the broom."

And in the bunkhouse, where a poker game was in session, Slim Mitchell said derisively, "Now we're sunk for sure — workin' for a shemale."

Fayette frowned and went on. Monk Rodenbaugh, he decided, had gone too far with his opinions. Rodenbaugh needed trimming down to size.

An outburst of raucous laughter came from the bunkhouse, and Fayette made his guess as to the source of that hilarity. They were a tough bunch, this crew he'd bought to Spur — the toughest collection of culls east or west of the Pecos. Monk Rodenbaugh had been run out of Texas for killing a bartender with his fists. Slim Mitchell, who was scarcely dry behind the ears, had two notches on his gun. Single-O Smith, Breed Santana and Limpy Peebles were wanted in Texas for murder, and Faro Pratt had held up the Senate Saloon in El Paso. English Joe and Sam Arbuckle were just outcasts, as far as Fayette knew, but it was significant that Arbuckle, who'd got a bullet in his side two days after coming here, insisted on staying in the crew quarters instead of being bedded down with the wounded pair of Spur riders at the house.

"Don't want no damn shemales fussin' with me," Arbuckle had declared crustily. "What Doc Nelson and the boys can't do for me I'll go without."

Like to like, Fayette reflected, and nearing the corral, heard the soft tinkle of English Joe's music box over by the gate. Then the Britisher said pleasantly,

"Greetings, friend Jim."

"Monk run you out of the bunkhouse again?" Fayette inquired, unsaddling the horses.

"Yes — and no," the Englishman replied. "Monk offered to engage me in a contest of fists, using only one hand to accomplish the task. But I rejected his offer and came out here to enjoy a spot of music instead."

Fayette grinned. Nothing seemed to faze English Joe. If he had pride, it was buried deep. He seemed to have no regrets for the past, nor any worry for the future.

Turning the horses into the corral, Fayette said:

"Monk is getting too big for his breeches. In fact, he's bulging over 'em."

"He's a gross and unlikeable person," Joe declared; "as the Persian poet once put it —

'Down man's successive generations rolled,
Of such a clod of saturated earth,
Cast by the Maker into human mould.' "

"Just so," Fayette agreed, and grinned. But he wasn't grinning when he stepped into the bunkhouse and said, "Monk, I don't like your remarks about Miss Shannon."

Rodenbaugh eased his chair back from the table. The other three players — Slim Mitchell, Limpy Peebles and Faro Pratt — laid down their cards. And over on his bunk, Sam Arbuckle hunched up on one elbow.

"So you didn't like it?" Rodenbaugh said slowly, with deliberate insolence. "That's too bad, Fayette!"

Limpy Peebles, a dwarfish little rider with one short leg, chuckled gleefully. He nudged Slim Mitchell and said, "Monk smells raw meat."

Rodenbaugh got up and walked over to Fayette. "Just what in hell was you figgerin' to do about it?" he demanded tauntingly.

There was a leering, eager grin on Rodenbaugh's thick lips. The lust for battle was hot in his eyes, and he held his big fists like clubs cocked for swinging. His broad bulk outweighed Fayette by a good fifty pounds, and every man in this room knew his reputation as a barroom bruiser.

"Are you deaf?" he demanded, hugely enjoying Fayette's seeming reluctance to fight.

Instead of answering, Fayette glanced at the watching men and said, "Move that table back against the wall, and look out for the lamp."

Then he hit Monk with a snapping left to the belly and followed it with a right to the brawny one's jaw.

The smashing swiftness of that attack caught Rodenbaugh unprepared. It rocked him back on his heels and brought a bellow of rage from his snarling lips. His huge arms came up, blocking off Fayette's second barrage of blows. He shouted, "Here's where you git your needin's, Fayette!" and charged with the brute force of an enraged bull.

For a long interval, while the impact of fists thudding against flesh ran sharp and chocking through the bunkhouse, they stood toe to toe, slugging it out, grunting and sweating, trading blow for blow.

"Bust him down, Monk — bust him down!" Limpy Peebles yelled joyously.

And when Fayette finally took a backward step, Sam Arbuckle called from his bunk, "Grab holt of him, Monk, or he'll run out on you."

But Fayette wasn't running. He was using his head as well as his hands — knowing that his only chance of winning was to catch Rodenbaugh off balance. No light, lean-bodied man could last long standing toe to toe with Monk Rodenbaugh. There was too much weight behind

Monk's ponderous arms. One full-swung smash could cave in a man's ribs if it landed squarely.

Whirling in midstride, Fayette dodged swiftly around Rodenbaugh and tried to target his bulging jaw. The big rider ducked the blow, but Fayette slid in close and slugged Monk's midriff with two sledging smashes that brought a gusty grunt from Rodenbaugh's bloody lips.

Then, as Fayette circled again, he saw faces at the doorway — girls' faces, with shocked eyes and tight pressed lips.

Accepting Chinee Charlie's invitation to have a cup of coffee, Gail was sitting at the kitchen table with Belle when she heard a commotion over at the bunkhouse and heard someone yell, "Here's where you git your needin's, Fayette!"

That bellowing threat sent Gail to the doorway, and the unmistakable sounds of fighting drew her across the yard despite Belle's excited admonition, "Gail, you shouldn't go over there!"

Gail knew that. She had grown up with the knowledge that bunkhouses were forbidden territory to womenfolk. But something stronger than reason, or habit, drew her there now. It wasn't mere curiosity either for she'd seen several fist fights and been sickened by them. Yet she hurried to this one, and Belle was close behind when Gail stopped at the doorway.

It was a startling sight — a gory, brutal sight. There was blood on Jim's forehead where his black hair shagged down in disorder; his sweat-glistened face held an expression of sheer savagery as he lanced blood-smeared fists at the other man's face. She heard Jim grunt as a blow knocked him sideways, and saw red welts on his chest where the shirt was ripped open.

"That's Monk Rodenbaugh he's fighting!" Belle Nelson exclaimed. "Monk will kill him!"

And so it seemed, for Rodenbaugh loosed a trumpeting roar and charged Fayette with a two-fisted attack that sent Jim staggering back on his heels. Gail saw Rodenbaugh hit him in the face, the meaty *plop* of the blow making her shudder. She thought Jim was going down; he fell back against a bunk and seemed to sway on the verge of collapse.

"You got him, by Heaven!" a man yelled exultantly as Rodenbaugh moved in for the kill. "He's all propped for choppin', Monk!"

Gail shouted, "Dodge, Jim — dodge!"

It was an instinctive thing, that warning, born of dread and a fervent desire to have Jim escape those oncoming fists. But he didn't dodge. He lifted a boot, caught Rodenbaugh in the stomach and jolted him back. Then he slid around Monk, and as the big man turned, Jim hit him on the jaw, just below his left ear.

That single, solid blow seemed to daze Monk Rodenbaugh. His lips sagged open and he stood there stupidly swinging his fists like a man shadow-boxing. Fayette stepped in close; he smashed lefts and rights to Rodenbaugh's face, rocking Monk's head back and forth with each thudding impact. Then, measuring with deliberate calculation, Jim targeted Rodenbaugh's jaw with a tremendous blow. Whereupon Monk went down, loosing a yeasty sigh as he hit the floor.

Someone behind Gail said, "Good trimming, friend Jim!"

A gaunt, bleary-eyed man with a little music box in one hand eased past her and went inside, saying, "An excellent piece of trimming, indeed!"

Gail glanced at Fayette and watched him wipe his bloody knuckles on his chaps. The savage expression was gone from his face now, but there was a rash, taunting note in his voice when he asked, "Anybody else want to give me a whirl?"

His eyes were sleet-grey in the lamplight. They were sharp and hard and cold as ice. He peered at each man in turn, and when no one spoke, he said gruffly, "You, Jim, go fetch a bucket of water and give this ape-faced fool a bath."

Then he turned Rodenbaugh over, using his boot to accomplish this chore. The big man's face was a bloody pulp, and when those smashed, sagging lips uttered a wheezy groan, Belle Nelson exclaimed, "How dreadful!" and started for the house.

Gail went with her, feeling a little sick, and recalling the sheer savagery she'd seen in Jim's face, was sorry she'd come to the bunkhouse at all. There was something brutal and merciless in the way he'd pounded Monk Rodenbaugh down; something closely akin to the cruelty she'd seen in Red Bastable's face the day he'd beaten Jim in Reservation.

Then, as Gail followed Belle to the kitchen stoop, she saw Keith Fabian step from a buggy in front of the house. He called, "Gail — Gail darling," and taking off his hat with his habitual courtesy, hurried towards her. His blond, almost yellow hair was like a golden helmet in the door-way lamplight, and his face seemed even handsomer than Gail remembered it. He took her in his arms, kissing her briefly, and said, "I came as soon as the stage driver told me what had happened."

Then he held her at arm's length, gazing down into her face like a man viewing a re-covered treasure. "You're beautiful!" he ex-claimed.

"Even with this scratch on my face?" Gail asked and, for some unaccountable reason, felt like crying. Tears welled into her eyes, and the next thing she knew, she was sobbing against Keith's shoulder and he was saying: "Go ahead, honey, have your cry out. Then we'll leave this place and never come back to it."

That startled Gail. She drew back, saying, "But I've got to save Spur."

"It's already lost," he declared gently, and wiped her eyes with his handkerchief. "There's nothing left here but grief and gore."

Chapter XIV

On his way to the foreman's shack diagonally across the yard, Jim Fayette saw Fabian take Gail in his arms — heard the young banker exclaim, "You're beautiful!" They made a pleasant picture, standing there in the shaft of lamplight from the kitchen window — a romantic picture. But Fayette took no pleasure in watching it. Going on into the shack, he lit the bracket lamp and, building a fire in the potbellied stove, put on a pan of water to heat. Then he studied his reflection in the dusty mirror above the washstand and smiled self-mockingly. Monk's big fists had hammered his body aplenty, but that bloody gash on his forehead was the only visible mark of the fight.

Presently, when he'd soaked his sore knuckles in hot water, washed blood and sweat-streaked dust from his face and changed his shirt, Fayette quartered across the yard. Gail and Fabian had gone inside, but Belle Nelson was on the front gallery. She called softly, "Hello, Jim."

There was a plain note of invitation in

146

her voice. And she looked lonely, sitting there in the moonlight. Fayette asked, "Too crowded for you inside, Belle?"

She shrugged and smiled faintly, saying: "I've got the blues tonight. I've got them real bad, Jim."

The muted tinkle of English Joe's music box sounded over by the windmill. Fayette nodded towards the Englishman and asked, "Want me to call him over to serenade you, Belle?"

"No. He reminds me of Dad — always talking like a gentleman, and drinking like a hog at a swill trough," she complained. "Dad could have been a great surgeon if it hadn't been for the booze."

Her heart-shaped face held a wistful appeal, and she seemed to want his company, but Fayette said: "I'm on my way to supper. I'm hungrier than seven Sonora steers."

"I'll probably be here when you get through eating," Belle murmured suggestively.

"All right," Fayette said, and guessing that she had also witnessed the reunion scene, understood why she was feeling so blue. Belle Nelson was uncommonly frank for a woman; she showed her feelings without attempting to hide them, and there were folks in Reservation who called her brazen. But she had volunteered her services here when a nurse was badly needed. Pop Pettigrew and Banjo Jones didn't consider her brazen. Those two remaining members of Spur's original crew considered her a top-hand angel of mercy.

When Fayette passed the kitchen window, he heard Keith Fabian declare: "They'll desert you when the going gets tough, Gail. They're just riff-raff — and you know what Jim Fayette was when you first met him. Well, he hasn't changed. He's still a tinhorn gambler and a gunhawk to boot."

This much Fayette heard without intending to eavesdrop. But he halted just beyond the window and deliberately listened to the rest of it, hearing Gail ask, "What makes you so sure he hasn't changed, Keith?"

"Fayette proved it during the three days he was in Reservation after bringing his beef herd to town," Fabian declared. "He played poker every night and won consistently. The last night, after he'd cleaned out most of the players at the Belladonna, he accepted Pat McGurk's invitation to a private game and made another win. No amateur poker player would have that much luck, Gail. He's a tinhorn pure and simple."

Then Gail's voice, edged with irony: "He may be a tinhorn, Keith, but I doubt if he's pure, and I'm almost certain he's not simple."

Whereupon Fayette grinned, and going around to the kitchen doorway, asked, "How's chances for some chuck, Charlie?"

"Velly good," the cook declared with rare good humor, and motioned to the long table where Gail sat with Fabian. "Go ketchum, Mista Jim."

Gail smiled, said, "You must be starved after your strenuous exercise," and glanced at his bruised knuckles.

When Fabian nodded a wordless greeting, Fayette returned it in kind, and proceeded to pile his plate with food.

"What was the fight about?" Gail inquired.

"Just a little difference of opinion," Fayette drawled. "Monk wasn't sure I was foreman."

Gail said censuringly: "Well, you dissolved his doubts, and most of his face, Jim. I suppose he'll leave and take others away with him."

"No," Fayette disagreed. "Rodenbaugh won't quit."

"But you beat him unmercifully, didn't you?" Fabian demanded. "Gail says his face looked as if it had been tromped by a shod bronc."

"I don't think he'll quit, regardless," Fayette said bluntly.

"Have you talked with him since he regained consciousness?" Gail inquired.

Fayette shook his head. Whereupon Fabian said positively, "I'll bet a hundred dollars Rodenbaugh quits."

"Make it a thousand," Fayette suggested, and when Fabian's eyes blinked, Fayette added, "Make it two thousand, and I'll give you odds of three to two."

A slow flush crept into Fabian's cheeks, turning his bland face ruddy. "Have you got three thousand dollars?" he inquired doubtfully.

"In my money belt," Fayette informed him. "And I'll take a banker's word for your two thousand — or a cheque, if you've got one handy."

Gail glanced at Keith, seeing the excitement in his eyes and wondering at it. Keith was no part of a gambler; so far as she knew, he'd never played a game of poker in his life. She was surprised that he would give such a fantastic proposal a moment's consideration. It was inconceivable that a banker — even a young, handsome banker — would think of betting two thousand dollars with a man he'd accused of being a tinhorn. And Jim, Gail decided, was exactly that. It showed in the nerveless, casual way he waited for Keith to decide, as if it were a trivial matter needing no further discussion.

Even then, knowing that Keith was actually considering the proposition, Gail was confident that he'd refuse it. Jim began to pour himself a second cup of coffee; then, seeing that her cup was empty, asked, "Have another?"

"Yes, thanks," Gail said, and as their glances met, she felt a curious reaction. There was no hint of a smile on his face, and his lips were entirely sober; yet his eyes seemed to hold a secret amusement that was like sardonic laughter.

And then Keith surprised her completely. For he declared, "I'll take your bet!"

Whereupon Jim extended his hand, saying quietly, "I'm laying three thousand against your two that Monk Rodenbaugh won't quit."

Gail watched in silent astonishment as the two men shook hands. They were as different as they could be. Keith's light hair and broad, expressive features were in direct contrast to Jim's shaggy black hair and darkly inscrutable face. And there was an even greater contrast in the ways of their thinking, for Keith was a staunch believer in the principles of law and order and legal procedure, as her father had been. It was utterly astounding that these two should be shaking hands on a five-thousand-dollar bet. But they were!

Fayette glanced at Chinee Charlie, who sat over the stove. "I'd like to have you go to the bunkhouse and tell Monk Rodenbaugh to come here *muy pronto*," he said.

"Cholly go," the cook acknowledged, and padded outside.

As if bolstering his courage, Keith said: "Rodenbaugh will quit. I wouldn't be surprised if he's packing his war bag right now. Those drifters won't stand for being beaten up by a foreman. They don't like work that well."

"So?" Fayette mused, and leisurely built a cigarette. When Rodenbaugh's beefy face appeared in the doorway, Jim asked, "When are you quitting, Monk?"

It was, Gail realised instantly, the fairest form in which the question could have been asked. In fact, it was giving Keith a trifle the best of it, for Jim's words made it appear that he expected Rodenbaugh to leave.

The big rider gingerly thumbed his bruised jaw. He peered at Fayette through swollen, discoloured eyes and stood in scowling silence for a long moment. Then, with his voice coming thick and lisping through battered lips, he growled, "You think you're tough, don't you, Fayette — tougher than all git out?"

"Mebbeso," Fayette said.

Gail saw a fast-forming smile ease Keith's lips, and felt strangely sorry for Jim. Three thousand dollars was a big loss, even for a brash, high-stake gambler who handled money as if it were horse feed.

"Well," Rodenbaugh muttered, and in the moment he searched for words, Keith chuckled confidently.

"Well," Monk said, "you got good reason to think you're tough, Fayette. It takes a tol'able tough galoot to bust me down."

For a hushed instant, as understanding banished Fabian's confident smile, the banker's eyes showed a plain puzzlement. Then he demanded, "Aren't you quitting?" and stared unbelievingly as Rodenbaugh shook his head.

Gail glanced at Jim then, expecting to see him grin. But his expression didn't change and there was no sign of exultation in his voice when he said, "That's all I wanted to know, Monk."

Rodenbaugh went back to the bunk-house and Fabian declared: "I don't understand it! The man takes an unmerciful beating, and then, instead of quitting, practically licks the hand that beat him!"

"A queer breed, renegades," Fayette drawled.

That didn't explain a thing to Keith Fabian. He said again, "I don't understand it at all."

Then he produced a cheque book and, quickly making out an order on his bank for two thousand dollars, handed it to Fayette with a smile. "You win, without the slightest chance for an argument," he declared.

That pleased Gail immensely. It was fine to see that Keith was a good sport, even though he'd been so hugely surprised and disappointed. Cold-eyed gamblers weren't the only ones who could lose graciously, Gail reflected. Jim could have lost no better.

Fayette was walking towards the doorway, when Gail asked, "Do you think the crew will stick, Jim, through thick and thin?"

"No," he admitted. "Not all of them."

"Then how do you expect to drive three hundred steers to Tonto Junction and fight Bootjack all the way?" Fabian demanded.

Instead of answering, Fayette said laconically, "I thought I was working for Gail."

"You are," Fabian said hotly, "or at least you're supposed to be, according to her dead father's instructions. But I am advising her, which is my privilege."

"It is," Fayette agreed. "It sure as hell is. You stay right here and advise her to your heart's content."

Whereupon he went outside and walked around to the front, where Belle was sitting. Then, as he glanced at the livery rig that Fabian had brought from town, Fayette had a sudden inspiration.

Stepping close to Belle, he asked, "How'd you like to leave here right now?"

"And go back to town?" she asked, puzzled.

"Yeah."

"I'd like to, Jim. But what about Pop and Banjo? They still need care."

"Gail can take your place as nurse. In fact, it's just what she needs — something to keep her occupied."

That did it. "I'll go!" Belle exclaimed. "I'll get my things and be out in a jiffy!"

A few moments later, as the buggy rolled

out of the yard, Keith Fabian shouted, "Where are you going with that rig?"

"To the Belladonna for a game of poker," Fayette called back and, urging the horse to a faster pace, added: "I feel lucky tonight! Awful lucky!"

Fabian glanced at Gail, who stood with him on the gallery. "What colossal nerve — taking my rig!" he exclaimed in an outraged voice. Then he asked, "Why do you suppose Belle went with him?"

"Perhaps she wanted a ride in the moonlight, and didn't care who drove the horse," Gail suggested.

It wasn't a charitable thing to say, and she regretted it instantly. After all, Belle had done a splendid job, taking care of Pop and Banjo.

"Maybe Belle is worried about her father," Keith said. "Old Doc has been on another spree."

But Gail thought otherwise, and remembering how Jim had praised Belle for being an "angel of mercy," she felt vaguely disturbed. Perhaps this wasn't the first time they'd gone riding in the moonlight. Perhaps that was why Jim had seemed so unsympathetic this afternoon — so downright unconcerned about her feelings when he'd delivered the bad news. He had seemed almost a stranger instead of the man she'd once intended to marry.

And later, when Keith had decided to bunk for the night in her father's room, Gail lay awake thinking of many things — of Branch and her happy girlhood here, of what had happened in the few hours since she'd left the stagecoach, and of Keith's stubborn insistence that Spur was doomed.

But the thing she thought about before she went to sleep was the way Jim had driven off in the moonlight with Belle Nelson.

Chapter XV

It happened soon after breakfast the next morning, while Gail was in the back bedroom talking to Pop Pettigrew and Banjo Jones. Because Slim Mitchell was shaping a horseshoe on the blacksmith shop anvil, Gail didn't hear Keith's single shout of warning.

Pop Pettigrew lay propped in bed, his haggard, whisker-bristled face showing a thoughtful frown. "It's costin' Shad Harlequin a heap o' money to keep all them gunhawks on his payroll," he said; "cash money, which has been tol'able scarce hereabouts for two or three years."

He glanced secretively at his bandaged, bald-headed bunkmate, and Banjo drawled, "Tol'able scarce for a fact."

Gail smiled at them, not knowing what they were leading up to, but genuinely pleased to find them so nearly recovered. They were like old friends, these two; they'd ridden for Spur as long as she could remember.

Pettigrew said: "It ain't rightly none of our danged business, Miss Gail, but me and Banjo has been tryin' to puzzle out where Shad Harlequin dug up all the money to meet his payrolls. Bootjack beef ain't done no better than Spur's for the last couple o' years, and they've had to feed same as we have. Which means Harlequin should of run out o' *dinero* same as we did."

"And we got us a hunch," Banjo reported, his age-gnarled fingers tinkering with the bandage on his broken arm.

"What's your hunch?" Gail prompted, wanting to humour these loyal old riders.

Pop glanced at Banjo again, plainly seeking support. "You reckon as how we better tell it?" he asked. "She ain't goin' to like it none at all."

"Mebbe not," Banjo drawled doubtfully. "Mebbe we better keep it to ourselves a while longer, till we know for sure."

Pettigrew thumbed his bristly chin. "Seems like we should tell her, though — before it might be too late."

Gail thought they were joking then. She guessed that this was their way of having a little fun after monotonous days of convalescence. But she was wrong, and would soon know it.

"Tell me," she urged, "or I'll burst with curiosity."

Pop kept rubbing his chin. He glanced at

Banjo, peered at Gail and said finally, "Better close the door."

When she'd done it, Pop said in a low voice, "Well, me and Banjo got it figgered out that Keith Fabian's bank loaned Bootjack money to keep that big gunhawk crew going."

"No!" Gail exclaimed at once. "Keith wouldn't do that! Why, that would be the same as fighting Spur!"

"Well," Pop said stubbornly, "Fabian tried to talk Branch out of biddin' on that contract, which was the only chance Spur had to stay in business. He wanted Branch to just sit back and wait, and refused to lend Spur the money for a forfeit bond."

"If Fabian ain't backin' Bootjack, why would he try to talk your daddy into committin' bankruptcy like that?" Banjo asked.

"That doesn't prove a thing," Gail said emphatically. "Keith was just trying to keep Dad from getting into trouble. And besides, Keith's bank is short of ready cash."

"Shouldn't wonder," Pop said slyly. "Probably lent it all to Harlequin to meet payrolls with."

The mere fact that she was listening to such fantastic accusations made Gail feel disloyal to Keith, as if she were somehow implicated in suspecting him. Which wasn't so at all. Even though Branch had doubtless resented Keith's advice and his refusal to make a loan, her father would never have accused him of being in with Harlequin.

"Keith was just trying to keep Spur out of a fight it couldn't win," she declared.

"By grab, we still got a chance!" Pettigrew muttered.

"Me and Pop will be asaddle right soon," Banjo explained. "Then you'll see some fast beef gatherin' around here. Them bunkhouse bums Jim Fayette brought with him ain't much account, nohow!"

"How about Jim?" Gail asked smiling, "Is he much account?"

Pop snorted. "He's just a young gink with gun savvy — which was why Branch made him foreman. When it comes to cow work, me and Banjo will make Jim look like a town dude!"

Gail went to the door and opened it. "You may be right about Jim," she said, "but not about Keith."

She went out to the parlor then, and was wondering how long Jim's poker spree would keep him in Reservation, when she heard Keith call sharply: "You in the bunkhouse — come out empty-handed. I want no shooting here!"

That didn't make sense to Gail. What in the world was Keith talking about? Running to the doorway, she peered out and saw him standing in front of the gallery. Then, as her glance went beyond him, she stood staring in astonishment.

Shad Harlequin, flanked by Red Bastable and two hard-faced riders, sat his horse over there by the foreman's shack. Just beyond that group was another, six mounted men who made a compact ring around Limpy Peebles, Monk Rodenbaugh and Breed Santana standing with empty holsters. Diagonally across the yard, over by the blacksmith shop, two other Bootjack riders stood above Slim Mitchell's sprawled form, and three more riders sat horses behind a corner of the wagon shed — all these men holding guns in their hands!

Bootjack, Gail thought frantically, had struck in broad daylight without a shot being fired. Yet even then, with that astounding realization thudding through her mind, Gail didn't comprehend the meaning of Keith's words — until he called: "You're surrounded and outnumbered. Come out of there now, you fools!"

"We ain't takin' no orders from you," a

booming voice replied.

That, Gail guessed, would be the big rider she'd met up on Cathedral Divide yesterday — Single-O Smith. He and a couple of other men were evidently forted up in the bunkhouse. Gail walked out to the steps and saw Shad Harlequin glanced over at her. An exultant smile creased his hawk face. His tobacco-stained teeth gleamed yellow in the sunlight and he exclaimed, "Here's the queen bee herself!"

That, and the ripple of amusement from the men behind him, told Gail all she needed to know. Shad Harlequin was already gloating; so sure of victory that he could insult her on Spur's doorstep. Indignant, and desperately endeavouring to convince herself that Harlequin was bluffing, Gail went down and stood beside Keith.

"Why have they come here?" she asked him. "What do they want?"

Keith put an arm around her shoulders. "It's no use," he said soberly. "This is the end of something that should never have been started in the first place. You'd better tell those men in the bunkhouse to surrender, Gail."

"And damn quick," Harlequin called arrogantly, "before we bust this place wide open!"

"You wouldn't dare!" Gail exclaimed.

Harlequin loosed a hoot of scoffing laughter. "And why wouldn't we?" he demanded. "Your father put the outlaw brand on Spur when he sided in with Jim Fayette and helped him slaughter my cattle in Spanish Canyon."

"That's a lie!" Gail cried. "Your own men killed those cattle!"

Harlequin laughed again, sneering, derisive laughter. "Try to make folks think that, and see how far you get," he suggested. "The outlaw brand has been daubed on this place so thick that decent folks are calling it a renegades' roost!"

"And here's the proof," Red Bastable bragged. "Look at these noosedodgers we've ketched here. They're all wanted by the law — same as your foreman, who killed a sheriff in Reservation!"

"Jim Fayette is in town," Gail said, knowing how useless that argument would be, yet grasping at any straw that might delay the final showdown here.

"Fayette ain't the only one we're after," Harlequin declared. "We'll get him sometime, but we've already got a double-crosser who needs hanging right here and now. Ain't that right, Sheriff Drago?"

"Sure is," agreed a broken-nosed rider

with a star on his vest. He had already fashioned a hand-noose; now he flipped the rope over Breed Santana's bowed head.

The Mexican's hands were tied behind him. When Drago yanked on the rope, Breed followed the grinning lawman to the blacksmith shop and stood in the doorway while Drago tossed the rope end over a beam.

Harlequin said, "We'll fix Fayette the same way when we get him."

"And that ain't all we're after," Red Bastable gloated. He gave Gail a brazen, ogling appraisal. "Branch Shannon destroyed a lot of Bootjack property, same bein' cattle, and killed four of our men, besides woundin' others. Now you're collectin' payment, ain't you, Shad?"

Harlequin nodded and said, "Payment in full."

The brash hypocrisy of that brought an angry flush to Gail's cheeks. "Payment!" she cried. "You've killed my father and ruined Spur financially! What more pay do you want?"

"This," Harlequin declared, and made a slow, sweeping gesture with his right hand. "Spur — the whole caboodle!"

Vainly, desperately, Gail sought for some

way out. If only Jim were here, she thought, he'd know what to do — if anything could be done. She saw Breed Santana being lifted into the saddle of a held horse. The Mexican's swarthy face was turning a sickish grey, but he voiced no plea for mercy.

Gail looked at Harlequin knowing there was no mercy in him, yet asking for it. "Please," she called, "don't hang that man! Please don't!"

Harlequin chuckled. He said to Bastable, "She likes Mexicans — same as Fayette."

A Bootjack rider pushed Chinee Charlie out of the kitchen, shoving the old cook so hard that he sprawled full length in the dust.

"You brute!" Gail cried, and helped Charlie to his feet.

"She also likes Chinks!" Bastable exclaimed.

"Just a couple of old roosters inside," the Bootjack rider reported to Harlequin. "They're both bedfast."

Gail saw Slim Mitchell get to his feet, dazedly rubbing his head. Blood showed on his fingers when he lowered his hand. He glanced at the rope around Santana's neck and loosed a whimpering groan.

"Git over there with them other outlaws," Sheriff Drago growled, and booted Mitchell on his way.

Then Harlequin called to Gail, "Are you going to order them bums out of the bunkhouse, or shall we smoke 'em out?"

"Suppose I do," Gail asked. "What then?"

Harlequin laughed, hugely enjoying this opportunity to lord it over Spur's new owner. He winked at Bastable and said: "That El Paso school didn't learn her much, Red. She still don't savvy plain English."

"That's not necessary!" Keith Fabian objected, moving over to stand beside Gail. "Miss Shannon had nothing to do with the trouble, Harlequin. You've no right to take your spite out on an innocent girl."

The Bootjack boss peered scowlingly at Fabian. "You," he said, "know how this thing started. And you know how it's got to end. I've got the law on my side — which means I can do as I please. If your fancy-faced girl friend ain't looking for trouble, she should've stayed in town, where she belongs."

Then he added sharply, "And if you're half as smart as I think you are, Fabian, you'll keep your mouth shut from here out!"

Sheriff Drago came from the blacksmith shop with six sticks of dynamite cradled in his arms. "Here's somethin' that'll open the bunkhouse door in a hurry," he declared, a coil of fuse dangling from one arm. "And it'll spook that bronc into hanging Santana at the same time."

"Just the thing!" Harlequin exclaimed. "Breed and them other bums can all die together! They'll race each other to hell!"

Gail shivered. She glanced at Keith, and seeing the expression of horror in his wide eyes, knew he was convinced that Harlequin wasn't bluffing. Whereupon she called, "What do you want me to do, Harlequin!"

"Toll them jiggers out here empty-handed. Then pack up your duds and git. I'll give you one hour to vacate these premises!"

Gail felt Keith's arm tighten around her shoulders and heard him say regretfully: "It's the only thing you can do, honey. You've no choice."

"But he has no legal right," Gail objected. "It's — it's like giving him what Dad died to protect!"

Keith shook his head. "Branch went outside the law when he brought Fayette and those other renegades in here. He made a gunsmoke gamble — and lost."

"Make up your mind!" Harlequin ordered. "And it don't make no difference to me which way you choose. I'll get it all in the end."

Gail glanced at Santana. She felt the impact of his eyes and tried to guess the meaning in them. His face had lost its pallor and he no longer bowed his head.

Then, as Gail was about to bargain for his life with Harlequin, Santana smiled and said: "There ees no use to feel bad, *señorita*. Jeem Fayette weel feex those *bandidos muy pronto*."

"Fayette, hell!" Harlequin snarled, turning to face Santana. "I'll show you how it feels to tromp the air right now, Breed. And I'll laugh while you choke to death."

The Bootjack boss started towards the blacksmith shop, cautiously keeping out of range of the bunkhouse windows. "I'll lead the bronc out from under you, Mex — slow, so you'll get used to the feel of dying!"

Which was when a voice called sharply, "Stop right where you are, Harlequin!"

For a hushed instant Gail couldn't believe her ears. And she couldn't tell where the voice came from. But she recognised it at once — Jim's voice!

Harlequin whirled and peered at the house. Sheriff Drago also stopped in midstride, holding his cargo of dynamite at arm's length, as if suddenly afraid of it.

"Where the hell is he?" Red Bastable demanded, his eyes probing the ranch house roof.

"Up here," Fayette called, "and I've got a bead on Harlequin's belt buckle!"

None of them could see him. And neither could Gail. But she knew now where he was. And because it seemed utterly ridiculous for Jim Fayette to be using so odd a perch, she laughed hysterically. That giant cottonwood at the east end of the house was part and parcel of her girlhood days. A narrow ladder, fastened to the tree trunk by rawhide thongs, led to a boxed platform in its leafy branches — "the Eagle's Nest," Branch had called it; and Gail had spent many a summer afternoon playing there in the shady coolness. Now Jim, just returned from a gambling spree in town, was using a little girl's forgotten playhouse for a fort.

Gail glanced at Shad Harlequin, seeing perspiration grease his frowning face and watching indecision claw at his courage as he searched for the hidden gun that menaced him. His eyes, and the eyes of every man in the yard, were staring at the cottonwood. But they couldn't see Jim in all that high-towering mass of breeze-fluffed leaves, and they were wondering how well he could see them. It showed in the way they stood, with gun hands poised and bodies tense. Gail held her breath. If they all shot at the tree, some of their bullets would be almost certain to hit Jim.

Then, as if to prove how well he could see, Fayette fired a single shot. Dust bounced from the upturned brim of Harlequin's hat as a slug nicked it and *whanged* dangerously close to the dynamite in Sheriff Drago's arms. "Next one will part your hair," Fayette warned.

And from the bunkhouse came Single-O Smith's booming voice: "Hold 'em, Jim — we're coming out!"

"Now we hang the sheriff weeth hees own rope — maybe," Breed Santana suggested, and as if in celebration of that deed, there came the tinkling music of English Joe's music box playing a spirited polka.

That did it. Even though Harlequin, Bastable and Drago were the only ones directly in line of fire from the opening bunkhouse door, that unseen gun in the tree covered the whole yard. Harlequin dropped his gun without a word, only the savage scowl that rutted his face telling of his controlled rage.

"Rest of you rannyhans do likewise," Fayette ordered, and when this had been done, he called, "Now *vamoose,* Harlequin, and take your bully boys with you!"

Gail didn't see the rest of it. For tears suddenly blinded her eyes and a strange weakness made her seek support in Keith's arms. She heard horses go out of the yard at a run, and heard Keith exclaim in amazement: "He did it! He drove them off singlehanded!"

Then Jim's voice came to her, deep and drawling and a trifle tough: "Saddle up, you sashay sports! We've got a beef herd to gather!"

Chapter XVI

Jim Fayette was talking to Chinee Charlie at the loaded chuck wagon when Gail and Keith came out of the house. The banker said, "Congratulations on winning a brilliant bluff."

"It wasn't a bluff," Fayette muttered, tallying the provisions and bedrolls that had been piled into the wagon.

"But you were outnumbered ten to one," Fabian countered. "You couldn't possibly have survived all those guns if they'd decided to fight."

Fayette said: "Mebbe not, but neither would Harlequin. That made it even."

"How did you ever happen to discover the Eagle's Nest, Jim?" Gail asked wonderingly.

"Saw the ladder when I came up behind the house, which was after I'd noticed a lot of fresh horse tracks crossing the trail back yonder," Fayette explained.

Then he glanced at English Joe, who had finished harnessing the mules and was taking his place beside Chinee Charlie on the chuck wagon seat. "We'll camp at the spring below Latigo Pass," he announced, and eyeing the assembled riders, said, "Single-O and Breed will act as lookouts while the rest of you work the beef."

"Seems kind of late in the day to start a roundup," Limpy Peebles complained.

This sulky suggestion didn't mean much in itself. But it held a hint of mutiny and Fayette couldn't ignore it. So he said bluntly, "You ride like you're told, Peebles, or draw your wages right now!"

He shifted his glance from face to face and, coming to Monk Rodenbaugh, said, "That goes for the rest of you sashay sports."

"I ain't kickin'," Rodenbaugh said quickly.

And Fargo Pratt drawled: "Hell, no, boss. We like it here — so calm and peaceful and all."

"Then get started," Fayette ordered gruffly. Slim Mitchell adjusted his hat so it would fit his bandaged head, and yelled, "Open the gate!"

Whereupon he drove the *remuda* out of the enclosure and headed it north. The chuck wagon rolled from the yard, and the crew went with it.

"What a loyal, industrious bunch of

men!" Fabian said sarcastically.

"You know where Spur can hire better men?" Fayette inquired, and stepped into the saddle.

"That's not the point," Fabian snapped irritably and, turning to Gail, said: "Can't you see how hopeless this thing is? If by some miracle these renegades round up a trail herd in time, what chance will it have of ever reaching Tonto Junction?"

Fayette watched Gail's face, seeing the frown that turned her lips entirely sober; guessing at the conflict of tangled emotions that tugged at her now. For even though she cherished the memory of her father and had a deep-rooted affection for her home, she was in love with Fabian. You could tell that by the way she looked at him.

But because Fayette had already decided how this game had to be played, he showed no sign of sympathy or understanding. "What's it going to be?" he asked flatly. "Do we gather a beef herd, or don't we?"

Gail glanced up at him, her eyes urgently questioning. It was as if she were seeking something from him — some important clue that would influence her decision. The thought came to Fayette that her eyes were beautiful even when she frowned;

they were wide and warm and they did things to a man — queer, contrasting things that made him feel gay and sad at the same time, like listening to English Joe's music box.

Gail said finally, "Why are you so anxious to make the beef drive, Jim?"

"Hell, I'm not anxious at all," he answered. "I ought to be down at Border Desert right now, helping the boys fight off Bootjack raiders."

"Then why are you in such a hurry to get the roundup started?" Fabian demanded.

Fayette ignored the banker's question. He said to Gail: "Branch asked me to help him make the drive. His dying didn't change my part of the bargain — unless you want it changed."

Gail's eyes held a moist wistfulness now, and her lips were gently smiling. But Keith Fabian didn't smile. He said, "Gail, if saving this bankrupt ranch means so much to you, I'll buy the forfeit mortgage from Pat McGurk."

Fayette saw that register instantly. He watched relief show in Gail's eyes — relief and appreciation, as if she'd been waiting for such an offer and was glad that it had finally come.

A mocking amusement edged Fayette's voice when he drawled, "McGurk won't sell you the mortgage, Fabian."

"Why not?"

"Because he hasn't got it."

The surprise of that widened Fabian's eyes. "So Shad Harlequin bought it," he exclaimed frowningly, "just to play safe!"

"Mebbeso," Fayette muttered and, glancing at Gail, asked, "Any more questions?"

Gail shook her head, and when Fayette rode off at a run, he heard her call something that sounded like "Good luck, Jim!"

But he wasn't sure.

For fifteen consecutive days, while Fayette maintained a constant vigil against Bootjack raiders, Spur's hard-scrabble crew choused beef steers towards Singletree Spring. Out of brush-tangled canyons and twisting arroyos, of precipitous, rock-studded slants and through snagging thickets came the scattered survivors of the roundup which Branch Shannon had begun and which his death had interrupted.

From dawn until dark, dust rose in long, powdery fingers all across the northwestern corner of Spur's range, and toil-weary riders cursed stumbling horses; cursed the cattle and the dust and the bleak-eyed foreman who drove them so relentlessly; cursed and complained and threatened to quit; watched and waited for Bootjack to strike.

As Single-O Smith grumbled one day: "This ain't no roundup like I ever seen in all my born days! It's worse'n the ridin' I did for Jeb Stuart's cavalry!"

But they gathered a beef herd.

And they did it in record time. For when Gail rode out to Singletree Spring on the afternoon of the fifteenth day, Chinee Charlie declared, "Roundup almost finished, Missy Gail."

The cook gave her a cup of coffee and gestured towards the huge herd of grazing steers that were being loose-herded by a solitary rider. "Nine hundred ten head this morning. More now."

"Then the drive should start in a few days," Gail reflected, and calculated the remaining time before the delivery deadline at Tonto Junction — less than two weeks, and the drive would take eight or ten days.

"Does Jim say we've still got a chance to make it?" she inquired.

The old Chinaman shrugged. "Mista Jim velly fine fella, all samee Boss Branch —

talk little but think much."

And presently, when Gail rode out to where English Joe was riding slowly around the herd with his Mira music box tinkling merrily, she learned more about Jim Fayette.

"We have accomplished a month's work in two weeks," the Britisher announced proudly in his cultured voice. "It is scarcely less than miraculous the amount of work we have done, especially when you take into account the undebatable fact that a distinct sense of futility has accompanied this venture from the start. Yet I have never seen such riding, Miss. It's been like a continuous cavalry charge, *sans guidons*."

Gail eyed him wonderingly. It was incongruous that so shabby a saddle tramp should express himself in such scholarly fashion. "The men must have changed their attitude towards Jim," she suggested.

"Not at all," English Joe disagreed. "The men curse him roundly from morning until night. They even curse him in their sleep. And the threat of mutiny is like a smouldering ember ready to burst into flame at any moment."

"Yet they haven't quit," Gail reflected, completely mystified. "How do you explain that?"

The Englishman smiled and made an open-palmed gesture of futility. "It is inexplicable," he admitted. "Even Keats, the great bard and philosopher, could find no solution, for he wrote:

'How strange it is that man on earth
should roam
And lead a life of woe, but not forsake
His rugged path; nor dare he view alone
His future doom, which is but
to awake.' "

While Gail was absorbing that astonishing proof of English Joe's aristocratic past, he added: "The men say Jim Fayette has vinegar in his veins and a lump of ice where his heart should be. But they are wrong, Miss, for Fayette is actually a very human sort when you know him."

Gail smiled. This rider evidently didn't know that she'd once been engaged to Jim and should know him better than the men who rode for him. Recalling Jim's lack of sympathy or comprehension towards her lately, she said with thinly veiled sarcasm, "I suppose you know him exceedingly well."

"Quite," English Joe agreed. "I am a student of human nature, and I happen to

know that Fayette trounced Monk Rodenbaugh because Monk said you didn't look
like a lady."

"Are you sure?" Gail demanded, entirely
surprised.

"I am certain of it," he declared.
"Fayette is an unusually chivalrous soul at
heart — he's a regular gunsmoke Galahad
in disguise."

That information astonished Gail; the
part about Jim fighting Rodenbaugh because of her. And it pleased her immensely.
It seemed ironical that Jim, who had
shown her so little consideration that day,
should have fought a fist duel over so
trivial a thing as an expression of disre-
spect — Jim, who had shown her nothing
more than a frugal courtesy and seemed to
resent her being a lady.

She was basking in a warm glow of gladness at the thought, when Jim rode a limping, sweat-lathered horse up to the herd.
His eyes had a hollow, haunted look, and a
stubbly growth of whiskers bristled his
gaunt cheeks. Even his voice held a raw
tone when he called: "You, Joe — get a
move on! Keep those steers from drifting!"

Then, as the Englishman hastily de-
parted, Jim motioned for her to accom-
pany him towards the nearby *remuda*.

"Something wrong at the ranch?" he asked.

"No, I just came to tell you that Pop and Banjo say they'll be ready to ride in a couple of days. Sam Arbuckle is out of bed and itching to get on a horse."

"Tell them to stay where they are," Fayette muttered and, dismounting close to where Slim Mitchell held the saddle band, called: "Fetch me a bronc, Slim. This one went three-legged on me."

He was unsaddling when young Mitchell came trotting out of the horse herd with a big bay. "Hell, no — not that jughead!" Jim exclaimed. "Get me something built close to the ground — something that'll last out the afternoon."

"None of 'em will last the way you ride," Mitchell muttered crankily and turned back to the *remuda*.

Fayette gave the milling horses a squinting appraisal and called, "Dab your loop on that little rat-tailed sorrel."

Listening to the tough tone of his voice, and guessing how ruthlessly he had driven Spur's crew, Gail understood why the men cursed him; why they were on the thin edge of mutiny.

She said: "Jim, you're crowding the crew too hard. They'll quit if you keep it up."

The moment she spoke, Gail knew it was a mistake. But even then she wasn't prepared for the swift anger that flashed in his eyes.

"You take care of the cripples at the house and let me run the cow work," he growled. "Nobody quits without licking me first, and you can explain that to your yellow-haired banker sweetheart!"

"His hair isn't yellow!" Gail exclaimed indignantly. "And you've no right to growl at me, Jim Fayette!"

"I'm taking that right," he retorted. "I'll growl all I damn please."

Resentment flared in Gail like a high-soaring flame. The scornful, domineering insolence of him, talking to her like that! As if she were some painted percentage girl — or the flirty-eyed daughter of a drunken old medico. Remembering how he'd taken Belle Nelson off to town in the moonlight, Gail felt a curious, unaccountable sense of jealousy. And she hated herself for feeling it.

All this in the time it took Slim Mitchell to bring up the fresh bronc. Then, as Slim rode sullenly away, Jim said: "I don't feel like arguing with women today. Go back to the house, where you belong."

And this was the man English Joe had

said was chivalrous!

The man who was supposed to be *a gunsmoke Galahad in disguise!*

That was funny — so downright funny that Gail laughed — the cynical, mirthless laughter of disillusionment, of injured pride and disappointment.

"I'll go and come when I choose," she declared haughtily. "You act as if you owned those cattle — but they happen to be mine, which gives me a perfect right to express an opinion."

Fayette stepped into the saddle. He whirled the sorrel around and faced her. "If you don't like the way I'm running this show," he said gruffly, "get another foreman."

"Perhaps I shall," Gail declared. "Perhaps I'll pick one who'll show a little respect and common decency."

Fayette nudged back his hat. He rubbed sweat from his dust-peppered brow. And for a long moment as indecision plainly gripped him, Gail thought she had bluffed him down. But her sense of satisfaction was brief.

"All right," he muttered. "Pick yourself a new ramrod."

There was no anger in his voice now, and no resentment; just a sort of resigned weariness. Gail was wondering about that as she watched him ride off down the trail towards Spur. And she tried to smother a swift sense of regret by saying, "The nerve of him — growling at me!"

But the regret was still with her when she told Chinee Charlie what had happened and the old cook sadly shook his head.

"Mista Jim velly tired," he declared. "Tired all to hell. Him ride to Spur at nights and come back when Cholly build fire in mornings."

"You — you mean he's been keeping watch at the ranch every night?" Gail demanded.

Charlie nodded.

Whereupon the regret turned into something else — something that put a throaty throb in Gail's voice when she exclaimed, "Why didn't he tell me!"

The old cook went on mixing biscuit batter for a moment. Then he said sagely: "Men who can, do. Men who can't, talk."

Chapter XVII

Jim Fayette stabled his horse at Gilligan's Livery. Then, shouldering his duffel sack, he crossed Main Street and turned into Belladonna Alley. This was the supper hour, and McGurk's saloon was deserted except for Poker Pat, who greeted Fayette with outthrust palms.

"I'm playin' no more card games with ye, Jim. Niver again!"

Then the saloon-man glanced at the war bag and said amusedly: "So ye got yer fill o' fightin' for Spur? Well, ye should of stayed on the Border Desert where ye belonged. Lee Terwilliger rode through here yestiddy on his way to Montana. Said to tell ye Bootjack busted BD to smithereens."

That news hit Fayette like a slap in the face. "What happened?" he asked.

Poker Pat brought up a bottle and glass. "Terwilliger said it was a grand and glorious battle — while it lasted. Andy Kane's boys fit 'em from hell to breakfast and back again, choppin' down Bootjack riders

186

in bunches. But they was too many. Seems like Shad Harlequin took his whole crew down there — and lost plenty men before it was over."

"Who got away besides Terwilliger?"

McGurk shrugged. "Lee didn't say, and I didn't ask him. But he said Kane was dead and nothin' left at BD but a pile of ashes. When I asked him was he goin' to Spur to see you, Terwilliger laughed in me face. Of course he was a trifle drunk, but he seemed sore as hell because the crew was split instead of bein' at BD when the showdown came. Said if he didn't never set eyes on you agin' it would be three weeks too soon."

Fayette reached for the bottle, poured a drink, gulped it down and poured another.

"What d'ye figger to do now, Jim?" Poker Pat inquired.

"Just sit and wait," Fayette uttered, and emptied his glass again.

"For what?"

"For Shad Harlequin," Fayette snarled. "For the stinking, damned son who started all this trouble. And I'll blast him down, sooner or later. If it takes a year, I'll blast him down!"

The whisky felt good against the coldness inside him. Its jolt was like a clenched fist, knocking the weariness aside. Fifteen days of tedious riding with little or no sleep night after night had worn him down until the strain of it had rubbed his nerves raw and the need for rest clutched at him like a grasping hand. Yet now, with the riding finished and his responsibility ended, he couldn't relax.

"Ye look like ye'd been drug through a knothole with yer hat on," Poker Pat declared, eyeing him thoughtfully.

"Nothing wrong with me that a little sleep and a shave won't cure," Fayette muttered.

But deep down, where a man hides his private feelings, Jim Fayette knew differently. Sleep and a shave wouldn't cure the devils of discontent that had nagged him all the way from Spur, nor blot out the sense of shame that was like a festering sore inside him. He tried to tell himself that Gail had given him no other alternative than to quit. By Heaven, a man had his pride, didn't he? The ramrod of a renegade crew couldn't let a girl tell him how to run things. Yet all his thinking hadn't improved his feelings, for he hated the quitter role and hated Gail Shannon for forcing it on him. Or so he thought.

Now, with Lee Terwilliger's dismal message slogging through him, Fayette felt utterly defeated. Downing a third drink, he toted his war bag to the Palace Hotel and rented a room. Then he asked the clerk for an envelope, and was addressing it, when Belle Nelson came downstairs.

"Jim!" she exclaimed, plainly glad to see him. "What are you doing in town?"

Fayette sealed the envelope before answering. Then he said, "Just got a notion to sleep in a hotel bed for a change."

"You look awful," Belle declared, eyeing him solicitously.

She had a friendly way with her, this girl — a generous, comradely way. Fayette recalled the hasty kiss she had given him when they parted in front of this hotel the night he'd brought her to town in Fabian's rig. "Your reward for banishing my blues," she'd said.

Now he had the blues, the blackest blues a man had ever had. He asked, "Will you do me a favour, Belle?"

"Sure, if you'll sit with me on the veranda while I wait for Dad. He's due in from Bootjack, and I want to grab him before he stops at the Belladonna. I'm keeping him on the water wagon, Jim."

"Bargain," Fayette said, and accompanied her out to the bench at the far end of the veranda.

Belle asked, "What's the favor?"

He handed her the envelope, saying, "Ask Keith Fabian to deliver this letter the next time he goes to Spur."

A self-mocking smile twisted Belle's lips. "That will be tonight," she murmured, taking the letter. "Keith makes the trip every other evening."

After which she added flippantly, "Isn't love grand, Jim?"

"Wouldn't know," Fayette muttered. "Never gave it much thought."

Belle eyed him narrowly. "You did for quite a while," she contradicted.

Fayette shrugged.

"Wouldn't you like to have a home of your own, even a little place?" she asked, all the flippancy gone from her voice. "Haven't you ever met a girl who made you want to settle down?"

"One time," Fayette admitted. "But it didn't take."

Belle waited for him to go on. She absently fingered the envelope he had given her, then asked abruptly, "Say, aren't you going back to Spur?"

And when Fayette shook his head, she demanded, "What happened?"

Fayette gave his attention to fashioning a cigarette, and in this lingering interval Belle glanced thoughtfully at the envelope, seeing that it was addressed to Gail Shannon.

"So that's it," she mused, her voice low and warm with understanding. "That was the one time it didn't take."

Fayette lit his cigarette and smoked in moody silence for a time. Then he nodded towards the livery stable where Doc Nelson was getting out of his rig. "There's your dad," he said, and seeing Doc stagger, added, "Looks like he took on a few drinks at Bootjack."

Belle got up quickly, and Fayette went with her to the veranda steps. "I'll give Keith the letter," she assured him, and just before she turned away, she said soberly: "We're two of a kind, Jim. It didn't take for me either."

Fayette was thinking about that when he went up to his room and lit the lamp. Fate, he reflected, had tricked them both. It had cast them in second-class roles because Gail Shannon loved a yellow-haired banker who let her sob on his shoulder when the going got tough.

The room was warm with the day's trapped heat. And the whisky was beginning to take effect. When Fayette leaned over to take off his boots, a groggy, all-gone feeling struck him like a hard-swung club. He sprawled on the bed fully dressed and let a long sigh run out of him. He was remotely aware of footsteps going down the corridor, of hearing Belle say forlornly: "You're drunk, Dad. You broke your promise again."

And he could hear the old medico explaining thickly: "But Harlequin had two kegs of whisky, dear — two whole kegs!"

Whereupon Fayette went to sleep.

Chapter XVIII

It seemed like no time at all until Jim Fayette heard someone calling his name. When he opened his eyes, Belle Nelson was standing beside the bed, her face flushed with excitement.

"Wake up, Jim — wake up!" she urged.

Fayette shook his head groggily. "I'm awake," he muttered. "What's all the fuss about?"

"Dad just told me he heard Harlequin talking about a raid at Spur tonight!"

That banished the last strand of grogginess from Fayette's sleep-drugged senses. It brought him off the bed instantly and made him reach for his gungear and hastily strap it on.

"What time is it?" he demanded.

"A quarter past eight," Belle informed him. "Dad says the Bootjack bunch are all fired up with booze and wanting revenge for the riders they lost at Border Desert. They plan to smash the beef herd first, then go on to the ranch and take it over."

Fayette grabbed his hat and asked, "Did

Fabian go to Spur this evening?"

"Yes," Belle said worriedly. "That's why I want you to warn them in time, Jim. I — I don't want anything to happen to Keith."

The irony of that brought a cynical smile to Fayette's lips as he hurried to the doorway. Even though Belle couldn't have the banker, she feared for his safety. And he was feeling the same way about Gail. They were both playing second fiddle, both prodded by the same stabbing apprehension for people who didn't want them. As he was going downstairs, Belle called, "I'll pour some black coffee into Dad and bring him to Spur — in case he's needed."

"Good idea," Fayette said, marvelling at such straight thinking in spite of her fear and excitement.

Hurrying to the livery stable, Fayette saddled the rat-tailed sorrel and thanked whatever guardian angel had caused him to pick out a good horse at the *remuda* this afternoon. No telling what time Harlequin's bunch would make their raid; they might intend to accomplish their grisly job before moonrise, in which case they'd be riding towards Spur right now.

Fayette rode out of town at a run. He tried to recall what time the moon had risen last night, and guessed it was about nine o'clock. It would be an hour later tonight, but that didn't give him time enough — unless this sorrel had plenty of bottom. Yet even then, with apprehension prodding him like a sharp-rowelled spur, Fayette held the bronc to a steady lope; and later, when the animal began climbing into the hills, Fayette grimly slowed the pace. A horse had only so much run in him; the sorrel's endurance had to be rationed against the last long mile of this desperate race against bloodthirsty raiders bent on ghoulish revenge.

It was dark now, with a quilted blackness shutting out the shapes of thickets that bordered the trail. Night's coolness came out of the higher hills, and somewhere a coyote disturbed the vast stillness with its melancholy lament. For a time, while Fayette rode with the familiar smell of horse sweat and trail dust in his nostrils, he tried to shake off the sense of ominous foreboding that gripped him, and to tell himself that even if Shad Harlequin raided the ranch, Gail wouldn't be harmed. And when that failed to thaw the cold knot of fear inside him, Fayette cursed himself for a romantic fool. What difference did it make what happened to Gail Shannon? She'd shown nothing but scorn for him since the night he'd refused to sidestep the fight he'd inherited from Dobie Dan. Right now she was probably in Keith Fabian's arms, kissing him.

Fayette cursed and muttered futilely, "To hell with her!"

But later, when he topped Cathedral Divide and glimpsed the far-off twinkle of Spur's window light, he breathed a sigh of relief. No sound of shooting, nor of approaching riders. He would get there in time. Even though there wasn't a chance of saving the beef herd, Spur could be defended against a surprise attack. And Bootjack's crew had been whittled down plenty during the BD fight, according to Poker Pat.

Giving the sorrel a brief rest, Fayette rode on down the slope and, reaching the open flats, turned the bronc loose. He felt the animal's smooth surge of speed and knew there was plenty of run reserved for this final lap. Recalling Slim Mitchell's surly accusation that no horse could last the way he rode, Fayette grinned. There were a lot of things he didn't savvy, including women. But he knew horses.

Presently, when the sorrel had covered several fast miles, Fayette slowed him down, and by the time they reached the ranch yard, he was riding at a walk. No sense busting in like a flustered old maid late for prayer meeting, he reflected. He rode up to the house, saw Keith Fabian sitting alone on the front gallery and wondered why Gail wasn't with him, or if she was washing supper dishes in the kitchen, why Fabian wasn't with her.

The banker peered at him, flicked ashes from his cigar and said, "So you changed your mind about quitting."

Fayette ignored the sly scoffing of Fabian's voice. He rode on around to the kitchen door and, dismounting, stepped inside to deliver his warning to Gail. Which was when he saw Banjo Jones and Sam Arbuckle at the sink, clumsily washing dishes.

Even then Fayette had no inkling of what was in store. He asked, "Where's Miss Gail?"

Banjo eyed him with plain dislike, saying nothing. But Sam Arbuckle said, "She rode off with Pop Pettigrew right after supper."

"Where'd she go?" Fayette asked.

"Singletree Spring," Banjo said censuringly, "to try to keep the crew from quitting, like you did."

So that was it! That was why Keith Fabian was sitting alone out in front!

And the Bootjack bunch were going to raid Singletree Spring first — might be raiding it right now!

That realization cut through Jim Fayette like a sharp-bladed knife, and hard on its heels came another: a surprise raid at the roundup camp would be little less than outright massacre — there'd be no survivors.

Quickly then, and without waste of words, Fayette told why he was here. Then he rushed to the horse corral and was saddling a fresh bronc when Keith Fabian came running across the yard.

"Wait for me!" he shouted. "I'm going with you!"

A mirthless grin creased Fayette's haggard face as he leaped into the saddle. "This is no buggy-ride," he snarled derisively. "And Singletree Spring won't be a healthy place for yellow-haired bankers!"

Whereupon Fayette rode out of the yard.

Chapter XIX

When Gail and Pop Pettigrew reached the roundup camp, the men had finished supper and were sitting around Chinee Charlie's fire, morosely silent. Even English Joe's music box was still.

It seemed fantastic to Gail that they should react like this to Jim Fayette's absence. Surely they had no affection for their ex-foreman — for the man who'd driven them so hard and so ruthlessly. Monk Rodenbaugh's face still bore the marks of Jim's fists, and all these riders had felt the bite of his bitter words. Yet now they acted like a bunch of downcast dogs abandoned by their master. It didn't make sense.

Breed Santana asked, "Per'aps Jeem weel come back *mañana* — maybe?"

"No," Gail said, and sensed the deep disappointment that single word brought to these frowning riders. "I'm making Pop Pettigrew foreman, and I'm depending on you men to work as hard for him as you did for Fayette."

There was a long moment of silence. Then Single-O Smith muttered. "I can't figger out why Jim would of quit. It don't seem fittin' that he should do a thing like that."

"Seems downright queer, him bunchin' it after sayin' any man wanted to quit had to lick him first," Limpy Peebles declared. "By Heaven, I don't think he quit at all, I think he was fired!"

Gail felt their doubting eyes, sensed their forming suspicion that she had discharged Jim. It had never occurred to her that these renegade riders would be loyal to the man who'd driven them to the edge of mutiny — the man they'd cursed, even in their sleep.

Then Fargo Pratt asked bluntly, "Did Fayette quit, or did you fire him?"

Which was a question Gail couldn't answer definitely. "I'm not sure," she admitted, and knew by the sudden hotness of her cheeks that she was blushing.

"What difference does it make?" Pop Pettigrew demanded.

"Plenty difference," said Single-O. "All the difference in the world. If Jim was fired, I'll take my time right now."

And English Joe said emphatically: "I subscribe to the same proposal. I'll not ride for an outfit that would treat a man of Fayette's capabilities so shabbily."

"But I didn't fire him!" Gail insisted. "Not really."

Doubt was a tangible presence at this campfire, the feel of it so strong that it was like a hard wind blowing, a cold, raw wind. It made Gail shiver. And it made her understand how close these men were to group desertion. If they quit now, Spur's last hope of survival would go with them. For unless this beef herd was delivered at Tonto Junction on time, the forfeit would be gone and Spur would belong to the holder of the mortgage — to Shad Harlequin, if he had it. And Gail was sure he did.

So she made a final appeal. "I'll pay every man a hundred-dollar bonus," she promised, "if our trail herd beats the deadline to Tonto Junction!"

She thought that would settle it. She thought the lure of prize money would make these hired gunhands sit up and take notice, would make them forget about Jim Fayette. But she was wrong and soon knew it.

Single-O Smith plucked a burning twig from the fire, his piratical face gleaming briefly as he lit a cigarette. "It ain't the money," he explained, exhaling a long drag of smoke. "A man can git along without money if he has to. He can make out, one way and another. But you got to have a good ramrod on a deal like this. You got to have a galoot that knows all the angles, or you're liable to git hurt bad. We had us a good ramrod. Now we ain't got him."

Which was when Gail pocketed all her pride and said: "I didn't fire Jim, but it was my fault he quit. I'll — I'll go to Reservation in the morning and ask him to come back."

"Don't reckon as how you'll have any luck," Smith predicted. "Jim only took this job because he felt sorry for your father. He's got no reason to feel sorry for you."

"Neither have we," Limpy Peebles said.

And Slim Mitchell added sullenly, "Never did like workin' for a shemale, nohow."

Gail turned away from the fire. Tears of bitter frustration welled up in her eyes. She felt ashamed — more ashamed than she'd ever been. It had been bad enough to pocket her pride — to humble herself before these renegade riders. But to be scorned by them . . .

Gail walked wearily to the chuck wagon and stood leaning against it, choking down the words of futile anger that formed on her lips. If ever a bunch of men needed firing, these Border scum needed it. But because she was fighting for her father's monument, she swallowed her resentment.

"Too bad — too bad," Chinee Charlie sympathized, and handed her a cup of coffee.

Pop Pettigrew came up and said dejectedly, "They'll run like rats from a sinking ship unless you can talk Fayette into coming back."

Gail nodded, took a drink of coffee and said: "I'll try. I'll do anything to keep Dad's contract."

And then she heard a running horse out on the flats, coming from the direction of Spur.

For a moment, as she stood listening to that beat of hoofs, Gail thought it might be Jim. That was the way he rode — hell-for-leather, the way old Dobie Dan used to ride. But almost at once she thought how senseless such wishful thinking was. Jim wouldn't be riding tonight. He'd be playing poker in Reservation, or sleeping. Perhaps he'd be calling on Belle Nelson.

But who was it? And why was he riding so fast? Surely it couldn't be Keith, who always used a livery rig for his trips to Spur.

And neither Banjo nor Sam Arbuckle was in shape to ride like that.

"In one hell of a hurry, whoever it is," Pop muttered.

And over by the fire Slim Mitchell exclaimed, "Sounds like Fayette, bustin' of the breeze, as usual!"

Yet even then, with a rising tide of anticipation in her, Gail couldn't believe it was Jim — until she saw him slide his horse to a stop. Then she exclaimed, "Jim!"

Fayette jumped down and led his panting bronc to the fire. "Saddle up, you sashay sports," he ordered. "Bootjack is going to pay us a visit."

His voice was harsh. But there was no excitement in it and nothing in his face to show he sensed the dramatic effect of this return. He looked, Gail thought, as if he'd been for a quiet ride to the ranch and back.

The men scrambled to their feet, one of them asking, "When is Bootjack coming?"

"Tonight — mebbe soon," Fayette said.

Abruptly then the camp was a beehive of activity. Riders grabbed up their saddles and reached for their ketch-ropes.

Fayette came over to Gail and said, "You and Pop get back to the house *muy pronto*."

Gail tried to control the welter of emotions surging through her — surprise and gladness at Jim's return, and a sharp sense of danger; of impending calamity and bloodshed. She tried to keep the excitement out of her voice — to ask calmly, "What are you planning to do?"

"I'm going to try to save this beef herd," he said quietly.

And at this exact instant guns began blasting north of the camp. Fayette grabbed Gail, pushed her towards a horse and said, "Ride — ride!"

And then other guns exploded to the south, to the east and west!

"They've got us surrounded!" Pop Pettigrew yelled. Gail felt Jim's fingers tighten on her arm and heard him say, "Too late now."

He turned her towards the chuck wagon and ordered, "Get under there quick!"

The rest of it was like a feverish nightmare to Gail, like a swirling chaos of noise and confusion — a maelstrom of blasting guns and stampeding horses and cursing men. She had a sharply etched glimpse of Jim jumping into the fire, saw him scatter its red embers with his boots. Then, as the firelight faded, there was only his voice rising raw and gruff against the tumult: "Bring the bedrolls to the wagon — we're forting up!"

Lead laced the air with its vicious whine. Horses pitched past the wagon, one shrilling an agonized whinny and collapsing so close that its flailing hoofs showered Gail with dirt. Shadowy shapes came out of the darkness, dragging bedrolls, piling them around the wagon.

Dust and smoke and Jim's sharp voice saying, "Here comes the beef!"

Gail heard it then — a rumbling roar that grew louder as she listened; a monstrous, thunderous, thudding roar that grew and grew until it filled the night. Gail felt the ground tremble beneath her and suddenly understood that the Bootjack raiders hadn't merely stampeded the herd — they were driving it towards this camp!

For a queerly suspended interval there was a vacuum-like hush here at the wagon. Then Gail heard Jim say calmly: "Wait till those steers get close. Then shoot low, and we'll split 'em."

"Maybe," Breed Santana remarked with sly humour. Prompted by an urge she couldn't define, Gail crawled from beneath the wagon and said, "Jim."

When he growled, "Get back down there where you belong," she stepped up behind him and stood so close that his tall form made a familiar outline against the gloom

— against whatever was to come. It made her remember the day he'd shielded her from that ambush gun on the ridge, and how his voice had kept her from screaming.

Finally, as the increasing roar rose to a high crescendo of awful sound, Jim's gun exploded. The compact group of Spur riders followed suit instantly, muzzle flame making a weirdly beautiful bouquet of orange flashes in front of them.

Gail glimpsed the ghostly faces of fear-maddened steers, saw a brute charge head on, so close that its wild eyes reflected the flash of blasting guns. For a frenzied, panic-stricken moment she held her breath. There seemed no stopping that wild-running leader, nor the steers behind it!

Then abruptly the big animal went down. Another bawled out its death bellow and collapsed on the leader's sprawled carcass. A third keeled over, and a fourth, forming a wedge that became a grisly barricade as more bullet-riddled steers piled up.

Gail heard English Joe exclaim: "Bravo! They're splitting!"

And she watched Jim's shoulders hunch as he shoved fresh shells into his gun.

Then a three-quarter moon rose above Cathedral Divide, flooding the flats with a mellow light that revealed the surging mass of stampeding steers — and the little group of men who were so valiantly turning that insane torrent of hoofs and horns aside. It was a sight to see — a sight to remember. Dust and gunsmoke made a swirling, acrid fog. Thunderous hoof-pound, the clash and clatter of horns, the bellowing of brutes being trampled to death — all merging into a hellish bedlam as grunting cattle plunged past the wagon in frantic flight for what seemed an eternity to Gail — until finally there were no more steers save the sprawled mass of dead and dying brutes directly in front of the wagon.

But even as the rumble of the stampede diminished, there was the sound of running horses out there in the dust-hazed distance, and then of Shad Harlequin yelling: "Ride the wagon down! Ride it down!"

And then it came, like a cavalry charge, with riders hurtling out of the moon-tinselled fog. Instinctively Gail dropped to the ground behind Jim, who was on one knee firing a Spencer carbine. She saw a rider go down, heard him loose a yelp of pain as he fell backwards from the saddle, and was vaguely aware of bullets whining close.

As suddenly as it had come, the charge ended. And Jim was pushing her beneath the wagon, saying: "That was only a warm-up. The next one will be different. You and Charlie keep out of the way."

Gail grasped his sleeve. "Be careful," she urged.

A ghost of his old grin quirked Jim's lips. He said, "Sure," and patted her shoulder and said in a softer voice than he'd used in a long time, "The trail herd is lost — but you won't lose Spur, regardless."

That calm assurance, and the intimate tone of his voice, made Gail remember English Joe's declaration. And it made her smile a moment later when she heard Jim ordering the crew to defensive positions around the wagon with all the rash toughness of a Rio renegade.

"You sashay sports wait for them to get close," he commanded, "like we did with the steers. We've got no ammunition to waste."

Chinee Charlie, who crouched close to Gail beneath the wagon, said, "Mista Jim velly good fighter with plenty know-how."

"He certainly is," Gail agreed heartily,

and peering out, saw men crouching behind bedrolls.

"They're comin' at us Injun style this time," Single-O Smith announced.

And then, with the sound of converging riders rising steadily from east of camp, the tinkling notes of *Serenade* came from the bedroll where English Joe was hunkered.

"Shut that damn thing off before I cram it down your scrawny throat!" Monk Rodenbaugh snarled.

But Jim Fayette said amusedly, "Leave him alone, Monk."

"Our ape-featured comrade has no appreciation of the finer things of life," the Britisher said sorrowfully. "What a pity!"

A strange, contrasting bunch, Gail reflected. Less than an hour ago they'd been on the verge of quitting. They had scoffed at her plea for loyalty. Yet now they were arguing about music in the midst of a last-ditch stand for survival.

Gail was thinking about that when Slim Mitchell demanded, "Ain't they close enough now?"

"No," Jim muttered, and for another long moment the Mira's gentle music merged with the increasing thud of hoofs. Then Jim snapped, "Dab it on 'em!"

Instantly the music was drowned out by

blasting guns — by the close pound of hoofs and the kill-crazy yells of Bootjack raiders bent on massacre. It made Gail shiver, that yelling. It was like the blood lust ballad of shrieking maniacs — like nothing she'd ever heard before.

Slugs smashed into the wagon box above, showering her hair with splinters. Ricochetting bullets glanced off metal parts of the wagon with twanging snarls of sound; they clanged into Chinee Charlie's pots and pans. And because Harlequin's riders were circling the wagon Indian fashion, the bullets were coming from all directions.

Gail peered through the dust, trying to identify Jim — and saw a tall man fall back from a bedroll, so close that one of his hands struck the wheel in front of her. The terrifying fear that it was Jim sent her crawling quickly out. Then, as she looked down at Faro Pratt's slack-jawed face and saw the bullet hole almost directly between the eyes, she felt a guilty sense of relief.

Pop Pettigrew, hastily reloading his gun, called, "Git back under the wagon, Miss Gail!"

Then Limpy Peebles collapsed with a grunting groan, and Pop added morosely: "We ain't got a chance. They'll whittle us down, one by one!"

Chapter XX

Jim Fayette shoved his last three shells into the Spencer's loading gate. He rested his elbows on a bedroll and peered out into the swirl of hoof-churned dust, taking time for accurate aim. Harlequin's bunch were still circling out there making vague, shadowy shapes except when their guns exploded. Fayette fired, saw a horse go down, and catching another rider in his sights, fired again.

This battle, he guessed, would soon be over. It had taken a lot of bullets to split the stampeding herd, and there was little ammunition left. He fired his one remaining shot, and missing, discarded the Spencer with a curse. Then he crawled over to Peebles's death-sprawled body, took the Colt from the little rider's clutching fingers and muttered, "Poor Limpy!"

He glanced beneath the wagon, where Gail was bandaging a bloody wound in Monk Rodenbaugh's right arm while Chinee Charlie held a tourniquet tight. A slanting ray of moonlight put a sorrel sheen on Gail's hair, and her long, dark lashes made twin smudges on the pale oval of her face. Remembering how she'd called his name during the stampede — how she'd stood close behind him without a whimper while steers charged head on — Fayette felt a compelling admiration. She was a fit daughter for the proud old cowman who'd sired her. Even now, with inevitable disaster looming close, she showed no fear, no excitement. He saw her slender fingers tie the bandage, heard her say reassuringly to Monk, "That will stop the bleeding."

Fayette turned back to the bedroll barricade, back to the grim task of making each bullet count. But the picture of Gail was a lingering image in his mind and the gentle run of her voice strongly affected him. She was the only girl he'd ever wanted. He had known that the first time he saw her, and had known it also when he lost her. Until tonight he'd believed there was no chance for him at all. Now he wasn't so sure. Something in her voice and in her eyes told him there might be a chance — and the thought of it sent a tumult of exultation rushing through him. He'd won her away from Keith Fabian once. Perhaps he could do it again!

He was thinking about that when Single-O Smith announced disgustedly, "I'm all out o'shells!"

"Me too," Breed Santana reported. "Per'aps now we weel have to throw stones at them — maybe."

Fayette pointed to Pratt's body and said: "Few left in Faro's belt. Split 'em between you."

"Then what?" Slim Mitchell whined. "We can't keep 'em off us without bullets."

Whereupon English Joe intoned, "The coward dies a dozen deaths; the brave man dies but once!"

That pompous declaration was punctuated by the thumping blow of a bullet against Fayette's left shoulder. A sharp splinter of pain spiraled across his back; then his arm went numb and there was no feeling in it. Fayette cursed softly, dejectedly, and at this moment caught a brief glimpse of Red Bastable's buck-toothed face as the Bootjack ramrod galloped past. Firing instantly, Fayette saw Bastable sag in the saddle a split second before an upswirl of dust screened him from view.

The almost certain knowledge that he had cut down Harlequin's foreman gave Fayette a brief and savage satisfaction. But at once he realized that Bastable's death was unimportant — that it wouldn't alter the final outcome here. For those Bootjack killers were bent on wipeout slaughter; they'd given notice of that when they surrounded the camp at the start, cutting off all chance of escape. This, Fayette knew, was Spur's last stand — and Gail's as well.

Grimly, with blood's sticky wetness sogging his shirt, Fayette waited for another close target. And he tried to banish the nagging vision that haunted him — the dismal, disastrous finale that would come when booze-crazed riders rushed this camp and a sorrel-haired girl died with the remnants of her renegade crew.

And then, with pain and futility closing in on him like a crushing vise, Fayette saw three Bootjack raiders go down as if struck by the same bullet; saw others wheel their broncs in swift retreat. He was wondering about that, and about the staccato burst of firing beyond them, when he glimpsed something that made him stare in dazed bewilderment.

He heard Single-O Smith blurt, "I'll be damned to hell!"

And Chinee Charlie cackled, "Ketchum plenty bullets now!"

But because Jim Fayette couldn't believe his eyes, those voices scarcely registered.

For he was staring at an apparition as ridiculous as a drunkard's dream. He was watching a livery rig careen out of the smoky haze with Banjo Jones supporting Branch Shannon's old Gatling gun on his hunched shoulders while Sam Arbuckle fired the chattering weapon at fleeing riders and Keith Fabian drove the galloping horse towards the roundup camp!

It was an amazing thing, an outrageous, crazy, unbelievable thing. Three men in a livery rig had turned the tide of battle with a surprise attack from the rear. And although it was the murderous fire of the Gatling gun that sent surviving Bootjack riders racing out of range, it was Fabian's devil-be-damned driving that had brought that gun through the ring of circling riders. And that, to Jim Fayette, was the most astounding part of this last-minute delivery from slug-slashed doom.

Dazedly, like a man not sure of his senses, Fayette watched Fabian jump from the rig and heard him call excitedly, "Gail, are you all right?"

Gail ran out to meet the banker. "Keith!" she exclaimed. "You've saved us all!"

"Keith's idee sure sounded loco as a hoot owl to me and Sam," Banjo declared.

"But it worked, by Heaven!"

Fayette got slowly to his feet, that motion bringing a grimace of pain. Gail was in Fabian's arms. But she wasn't crying, as she had done that night at Spur. She was smiling up at him, saying joyously: "You came just in time, Keith! We were almost out of ammunition!"

It occurred to Fayette that they made a singularly handsome pair, and that even if there had been a chance for him, there was none now. You couldn't try to take a girl away from the man who had saved your life. He felt no jealousy towards Keith Fabian. The banker had saved Gail from almost certain death. He deserved his reward.

Bracing himself against the growing weakness that clutched his legs, Fayette walked over to Fabian and said: "I told you this wouldn't be a buggy-ride, nor any place for a banker. But I was wrong, Fabian — all wrong."

Satisfaction glowed bright in Fabian's eyes. His cheeks, which had been chalky when he got out of the rig, were flushed now and he was smiling broadly. "Perhaps we were both wrong," he said. "I called you a tinhorn gambler, but you're no tinhorn."

"Just a gambler," Fayette muttered.

Then, as the other members of the crew crowded around for a look at the Gatling gun, Fayette eased out of camp unnoticed.

Shad Harlequin crouched close to his dead bronc. He cursed the riders who'd left him here alone, within a hundred yards of Spur's chuck wagon; alone — except for Red Bastable's body spraddled out over there in the moonlight. Harlequin's questing glance shifted from the excited group at the wagon. He scanned the surrounding terrain; weighing his chances of making a getaway. There was no brush on this level, hoof-tromped plain — no outcropping that offered shelter, save for the motionless mounds of dead horses and dead men.

Harlequin cursed again. He rubbed sweat from his face and heard a wounded rider moaning somewhere behind him. It would be a matter of minutes now until Fayette's crew came out here to investigate. They'd be wanting to tally the dead, to see whether Bootjack's boss was in that tally. Especially Fayette. That smartalecky son would come snooping.

The very thought of Fayette whipped up a high flame of rage in Shad Harlequin. Even though he'd succeeded in blasting Border

Desert ranch out of existence, Fayette was still alive — still making a monkey out of him every time they met. If ever a man needed gut-shooting, it was Fayette!

Harlequin's eyes caught the vague shape of a riderless bronc grazing off to the west of him. The bronc was trailing its reins and *moving slowly toward him.* A swift surge of hope came to Shad Harlequin. If he could get close to that horse without spooking it, he might make a clean getaway. And because he knew how surely he was doomed to death if captured, Harlequin fought down an impulse to rush at that riderless bronc. Then he remembered how Breed Santana had crawled away from the Calico Creek linecamp in broad daylight: *"Slow, like a lazy snake."*

And then, just as Harlequin started moving away from his dead bronc, he saw a man come from the chuck wagon — a tall, lance-lean man. Jim Fayette!

"Damn his hellish hide!" Harlequin snarled.

Insane rage shook him with a violence that made his hands tremble as he drew his gun. Fear and frustration were like bickering companions tugging at his reason. The almost overwhelming urge to kill Fayette was a monstrous, gnawing need; yet a gun blast now would attract those Spur riders over yonder. Their bullets would cut him to doll ribbons.

Harlequin peered at Fayette — at the limping, slow moving man who'd made a mockery of Bootjack power, who'd spoiled every deal. The Calico Creek fight, the Spanish Canyon fiasco, the raid at Spur two weeks ago and this one — all rigged into failure by one Mex-loving fool from Texas. And so it was now, with Fayette stalking that riderless bronc — spoiling the last flimsy chance of escape!

Hate burned like a feverish heat in Harlequin. It greased his face with sweat. It howled in his ears. Yet even then, with the need for revenge prodding him, Harlequin didn't fire at Fayette. A sly smile eased the angry pressure of his thin lips. There was still a chance to survive this deal — and kill Fayette to boot. For Spur's ramrod, now in the saddle, *was riding in his direction!* Harlequin took off his hat, holding it in his right hand so that it hid the cocked gun. This had to look like surrender when Fayette came snooping. It had to bring him close enough to give Harlequin a chance to gut-shoot him and grab the bronc's reins, a chance to kill and run and fight again — and win the whole caboodle.

Chapter XXI

Jim Fayette sat slouched in the saddle. The trivial task of mounting had seemed to tax the last ounce of his strength. The wound in his left shoulder was still bleeding. But it didn't burn now. It was like ice, freezing his whole body. He shivered and thought about Poker Pat's private bottle at the Belladonna. "A big drink is what I need," he muttered.

But there was one thing he wanted to know before he headed towards town — before he said good-bye to Gail and Fabian and wished them well. He gazed out across the moonlit flats at the sprawled shapes of fallen riders, and hoped fervently that one of them was Shad Harlequin. If Bootjack's boss had died here tonight, the fighting was finished and there'd be no more blood in the dust — no more broncs wandering in the dismal dawn with empty saddles. There'd be peace from Tonto to Border Desert, and homesteads on the Spanish Grant again. But peace had cost plenty.

Fayette frowningly tallied the price that

had been paid for peace: Dobie Dan and Branch Shannon in their graves, Faro Pratt's slack-jawed face with a bullet hole between its sightless eyes, Limpy Peebles's death-sprawled body — all the men who'd died at Spanish Canyon and BD. A hellish high price!

And it had cost him the only girl he'd ever wanted. But for Shad Harlequin's range-grabbing greed, there'd have been no heritage of hate, no reason for fighting like a Rio renegade — and no cause for a yellow-haired banker to save Gail's life and his own as well.

These were the things Jim Fayette was remembering as he rode toward a death-stilled shape. That, he guessed, would be Red Bastable. And then he saw a man get up from behind a dead horse, so near that he recognized Harlequin at once!

"All right, Fayette — you win!" the Bootjack boss called out, standing dejected, hat in hand.

Fayette straightened in the saddle, all the weakness vanishing from his muscles, all the sleety coldness thawing from his veins. His fingers hovered close to his holster and a rash wildness rose higher and higher inside him. This was better than having Harlequin killed in the dust churned confusion of wholesale fighting. This was personal — man to man — a chance to settle the score for Dobie Dan's death!

"Draw, damn you!" Fayette shouted.

But Harlequin just stood there, making no move. "Lost my gun when my horse went down," he replied.

Fayette shrugged. He said flatly, "Then I'll kill you with my bare hands," and riding close, was dismounting when he glimpsed a sly smile on Harlequin's flushed, perspiring face.

Instantly Fayette sensed a trap, the feel of it so strong that he was already drawing when the hat fell from Harlequin's hand, exposing the gun. Harlequin fired first, but because he was frantically endeavouring to grasp the reins with his left hand, that slug ripped harmlessly through the brim of Fayette's hat. Then Fayette fired twice in rapid succession, the gun so near Harlequin's chest that its muzzle flame flared brightly in his hawk-featured face.

"For Dobie Dan," Fayette muttered, and fired a third time.

He watched Harlequin teeter back, try to raise his gun and drop it. He watched rage rut Harlequin's distorted face for one fleeting moment, saw it fade into loose-lipped bewilderment — and heard Gail's frantic voice call, "Jim — Jim!"

All this in the time it took Shad Harlequin to flounder a few steps backwards and collapse with three bullets in his chest — to end the long and bitter war his greed had spawned.

Then, as if a sustaining hand had been withdrawn, Jim Fayette suddenly felt weak again — weak and sick and freezing cold. He was remotely aware of Single-O Smith's booming voice somewhere behind him, and others — Gail's voice, calling his name. He tried to answer, but his teeth were chattering. He turned to walk towards them. He was like that, a trifle off balance when his knees buckled beneath him.

Vaguely, as from a far distance, he heard Gail scream. And that seemed peculiar. Why should she be screaming now? The fight was finished, wasn't it? What in hell was there to scream about?

Then, for a queerly blank interval, the voices faded and he heard nothing at all.

Later — a long time later — Fayette heard voices again — heard Doc Nelson's whisky-husked voice saying, "He's lost a lot of blood, but the wound should heal in a week."

And presently, when Fayette opened his eyes, he saw Gail standing beside Branch Shannon's mahogany desk. That seemed strange. What, he wondered, was that desk doing out here at the roundup camp? Then, as his fogged senses cleared, he understood that this was Branch Shannon's room — that he was at Spur.

Which was when Gail exclaimed, "Jim — you've woke up at last!"

She came over and sat on the edge of the bed and asked: "Why didn't you tell us you were wounded? Why did you lose all that blood without saying a word?"

There was a plain note of intimacy in her voice. It was soft and sweet and entirely delightful to hear. And the scent of her hair was like a delicate perfume.

He said, "I didn't think it amounted to much."

"But you might have bled to death," she answered. Her eyes were smiling warmly, the way they had smiled in the old days, before Dobie Dan's death, before Branch Shannon had called him a Rio renegade. Something he saw in them now whipped up the same high gladness in him — made him reach out rashly and take her in his arms.

"Gail!" he said with a sudden rush of

tenderness. "Gail, honey!"

She said, "Yes, Jim?" and lips curved into a mischievous smile while she waited.

"Would you —"

"Yes, Jim?" she said again.

"Well, would you consider marrying a — a Rio renegade?"

"I've already considered it," she assured him happily. "And the answer is yes!"

Fayette kissed her then. He kissed her hungrily, in the fashion of a man savoring something sweet and rare and long desired. And because her lips were answering him frankly and generously, he knew there would be no more lonely trails for him. This was the way they had been that night long ago, the first time he had waltzed with her — like hunger and thirst and being drunk, all at the same time.

Afterwards, when Gail was arranging her tumbled hair, Fayette asked: "How about Fabian? Does he know how it is with us?"

"Yes, Keith knows," Gail said softly. "I think he's known it all along. He went back to town with Belle."

Then she added: "Which is where we'll have to go when you're able to travel. Keith says that even though Harlequin is dead, his heirs can foreclose the mortgage — and take Spur legally."

"Didn't Fabian give you my letter?" Fayette asked.

Gail nodded. "But he said it was from Belle Nelson. It's there on the desk."

"Maybe you'd better open it," Fayette suggested, and was grinning when Gail exclaimed, "Why, Jim — it's the mortgage!"

"Yeah," he drawled. "I won it from Pat McGurk playing poker that night I went to town. Put up my three thousand and Fabian's cheque against the mortgage. Pat says he'll never play poker with me again."

Whereupon Gail Shannon did a queer thing. She came over and sobbed against Fayette's shoulder and exclaimed, "Then we can keep Spur — you and I, Jim — for ever and ever!"

Fayette didn't wipe away her tears. He kissed them away.

The employees of Thorndike Press hope you have enjoyed this Large Print book. All our Thorndike and Wheeler Large Print titles are designed for easy reading, and all our books are made to last. Other Thorndike Press Large Print books are available at your library, through selected bookstores, or directly from us.

For information about titles, please call:

(800) 223-1244

or visit our Web site at:

www.gale.com/thorndike
www.gale.com/wheeler

To share your comments, please write:

Publisher
Thorndike Press
295 Kennedy Memorial Drive
Waterville, ME   04901